A CRY
at Midnight

The Shadow Creek Ranch Series

A CRY
at Midnight

Charles Mills

REVIEW AND HERALD® PUBLISHING ASSOCIATION
HAGERSTOWN, MD 21740

The author assumes full responsibility for the accuracy of all facts
and quotations as cited in this book.

This book was
Edited by Gerald Wheeler
Cover design by Byron Steele
Cover illustration by Joe Van Severen
Typeset: 12/14 New Century Schoolbook

PRINTED IN U.S.A.

00 99 98 97 96   10 9 8 7 6 5 4 3 2 1

R&H Cataloging Service
Mills, Charles Henning, 1950-
     A cry at midnight.

     I. Title.
                    813.54

ISBN 0-8280-1111-7

Dedication

To Dorinda,
the inspiration behind every word I write,
I love you.

CHAPTER 1

Lady in Distress

❄ ❄ ❄

Wendy knew someone, or something, was watching her every move. Early, her brown stallion with the white star between his large dark eyes, sensed it too and whinnied nervously.

"I know," the girl said softly as she patted the animal's warm neck. "He sees us."

Freshly fallen snow spread like a cotton comforter over the meadows and mountains of southwestern Montana, muffling the steady cadence of the horse's hooves as animal and rider headed higher into the hillside stand of cottonwoods. The air was still. The only movement to disturb the silent serenity was an occasional treetop avalanche of snow and the passing of the girl and stallion.

"Not too fast now," Wendy called. "You remember what Wrangler Barry said. Mustn't overdo. Gotta get your strength back slowly. Even though you feel like runnin' around, you gotta keep in mind how badly you got hurt by the River." The girl shivered, not so much from the cold, but from memories that still haunted her day and night. "The River," she whispered, speaking the word as if it was something to fear even now, months after the encounter with it that had nearly ended her life.

Early snorted, sending a swirling cloud of breath into the frigid air. Somewhere in his memory were fading visions of rushing water and feelings of absolute terror. But, unlike his human companion, he'd forgotten more than he remembered. For now, his thoughts centered on the apples he knew Wendy had hidden in her saddlebags. She always carried such treats on their rides into the mountains. They'd pause and gaze out at a particular magnificent vista or rest in a comfortable spot in the forest. It was at such times that the girl would offer the treats. To him, the River lived on only in sounds and smells he'd stumble upon purely by accident. In the horse's mind, each day was new and fresh, like the snow covering the landscape.

The two emerged from the grove of trees and skirted a silent meadow. Up ahead a rock formation rose majestically like a stone cathedral, complete with pine spires and granite bell towers. "We're almost there," Wendy said, adjusting the small backpack hanging from her shoulders. "He knows we're coming—he's been tracking us since Papoose Lake."

A movement among the rocks caught the girl's attention. She gently reined Early to a stop, and they waited patiently, frozen in place at the base of the formation.

"If you think you're fooling us, you're wrong," she called out, her voice much warmer than the air. "I brought Early this time. He's much better. But I can't run him for another month or so." Wendy stood in her stirrups and looked around, squinting into the harsh brilliance of sun on snow. "Wrangler Barry said he'll be as good as new come spring."

Suddenly a shrill scream pierced the silent meadow, the sound echoing into the valleys beyond. A low growl that seemed to vibrate the dead leaves on the bushes followed the scream.

Wendy smiled. "And Merry Christmas to you, too, Monty."

The sleek, intense face of a mountain lion appeared from behind a rock and gazed down at horse and rider. Early took a step back and whinnied, lowering his head slightly while pawing the snow with his left front hoof.

"Steady, boy," Wendy called, slipping quickly from the saddle. "That's just ol' Monty. I've told you about him a million times." The horse continued to back away, head swinging anxiously from side to side.

"OK, OK," the girl chuckled. "You can wait for me at the far end of the meadow." She fished a big yellow apple from a saddlebag and held it out for Early to see. "Here. Here's your treat. Now—"

Before she had a chance to finish her sentence,

the little stallion had grabbed the fruit from her outstretched hand, turned head for tail, and cantered away with a departing snort. Wendy watched him go with a broad grin on her face. "I guess horses and mountain lions aren't exactly the best of friends in Montana." She faced the creature crouching among the snow-crowned rocks overhead. "He won't go far. He'll just find a quiet spot, lean against a tree, and eat his apple like he doesn't have a care in the world."

The big cat sniffed the air and twitched his long, pointed ears. "Yeah," Wendy laughed, "I brought your dinner. Don't try to look so surprised. You've been watching us for the last hour."

Monty tilted his head slightly and moved his front paws in a sort of digging motion. "Relax, you silly feline," the girl chuckled, working loose the buckle of her backpack. "I've got all your favorite treats. A loaf of Grandma Hanson's whole-wheat bread, some cheese, a package of peanuts, and this"—she held up a large tin can—"tuna fish cat food. Yum, yum! Your favorite. The vet said I gotta teach you to like meat so that when spring comes you can catch a few mice and stuff, which I personally think would make a disgusting meal. But I'm not a mountain lion."

The big cat whimpered as he took a step.

"Still hurts back there, huh?" Wendy called, unwrapping the bread. "The doc said you may never get completely healed 'cause you broke too

10

many bones when the River tossed you in the hole. He did the best he could. Really. He said you're a lucky mountain lion 'cause you're not dead. But I gotta feed you twice a week until you can fend for yourself. I don't mind. You're my friend even though I know you're a wild animal and will never be a cuddly cat."

The rich aroma of tuna fish and peanuts reached the furry animal's nostrils, causing him to lick his lips in eager anticipation. The pain in his hindquarters kept him from joyfully pouncing on the meal waiting at the base of the formation, so he stayed on his perch, watching the young girl with the golden hair complete the preparations.

"Today's Christmas, you know," Wendy called, breaking large chunks of cheese into smaller, bite-size pieces. "We opened our presents this morning. I got this new hat from Debbie." The girl paused and pointed at the broad-rimmed leather head-piece pressed down over her ruffled hair. "You like it? Very fashionable. At least that's what *she* says. Hey, if it keeps my head warm, I'm thrilled. Dad got me a new lens for my camera, so I can take pictures of birds without having to walk up to them and scaring 'em away. Joey bought me a book on horses, and Samantha made me a flower pot. She said it was supposed to be something else, but she made a mistake."

The girl placed the collection of bread, cheese, peanuts, tuna fish, and a bright red apple on a newspaper and carried it to a small outcropping a few yards up the formation. There she put it carefully by a bush and backed away. "And this new green scarf is from my mom in Connecticut. She said I'm supposed to pretend it's her giving me a hug each time I wear it. I'd rather be hugged by her in person, but she'd have to have pretty long arms to reach me from Connecticut."

Wendy walked back into the meadow, then turned to the mountain lion. "Well, don't just stand there like an idiot. Your Christmas dinner is ready. Dig in!"

Monty sniffed the air several more times and then began making his way from his perch to where his food waited. Wendy watched him scramble among the rocks and experienced the same tender feelings she'd felt the first time they'd met in the dark, forbidding cave under the Bob Marshall Wilderness. The veterinarian had worked many hours on the injured animal, doing the best he could to fix the damage the River had inflicted on the young cat. It was only a month ago that Monty had been released from the wild animal hospital at Flathead Lake into her care. The doctor had been very specific in his instructions to her, repeating one message again and again. Monty was a wild animal, and could never be considered a pet. However, in order to survive, he'd have to have human help weekly, to make sure he was getting enough to eat. Wendy gladly took on the responsibility. After all, the mountain lion was more than a wild animal to her. He was a survivor of the River, something only they could fully understand and appreciate.

"Oh, I've got good news," Wendy called as she watched her friend eagerly begin his meal. "We're going to have a winter camp at Shadow Creek Ranch. Yup. For two weeks starting tomorrow. Got three kids comin' from Chicago and one from Orlando, Florida. I can hardly wait to see what the girl from Orlando thinks of Montana in December. Should be interesting!"

She paused, and a smile creased her face. "Ms. Cadena has been coming out to the Station every week for the last month to get us ready for our camp. She's the director of Project Youth Revival in Bozeman, and I think she's beautiful. Tells us lots of stories about when she and her mom traveled from Mexico to America. My dad always wears tons of aftershave anytime she comes around. I think they like each other, just like Wrangler Barry and my airhead sister, Debbie. It's all very sickening."

Wendy sighed. "I wish my dad still loved my mom, but he says that when she ran off with that bank president, it broke his heart." She looked at Monty for a long moment. "I guess bones are easier to heal than hearts."

The big cat took another bite of his meal and sat chewing, returning her gaze. He felt no fear of the girl. But an unseen barrier kept them apart. Monty looked forward to her twice-weekly visits, but he couldn't trust himself to approach her as he had in the cave. Her voice soothed him now, as it had then. He didn't understand what had come between them. All he knew was that she didn't belong in his world. And he had no place in hers.

With a final lick of the damp paper, the animal turned and climbed slowly and painfully up the rock formation, doing his best to keep his hind legs working in rhythm with his front paws. His stomach was full, and he felt sleepy. When he reached his favorite perch, he turned and gazed down at the solitary figure standing in the meadow. "See you in a few days, Monty," he heard her call.

Wendy watched her friend slip through a cleft in the rocks and disappear from view. Hurrying up the small incline to the bush, she retrieved the newspaper that had served as a plate for the big cat's dinner. Then she ran toward the far end of the meadow where Early waited, standing just inside the tree line.

It was Christmas Day. The Station would be buzzing with laughter and singing, and she didn't want to miss another minute of the festivities. Her duties were over. Now it was time to play—and to finalize plans for the winter camp. She chuckled. Imagine. A girl from Florida coming to Montana in the dead of winter! As she mounted her horse, she glanced back at the rock formation. Monty had returned to his perch and was watching her. Wendy waved; then, with a gentle kick, she and

Early retraced their steps through the winter woods to the valley far below.

* * *

"What do you mean you don't know where Shadow Creek Ranch is?"

The man at the airline ticket counter shrugged. "Sorry, ma'am. There are hundreds of ranches in this part of Montana."

"I know that," the woman stated. "But certainly there's only one with such a name. And it's supposed to be near Bozeman." She looked around. "This is the Bozeman airport, isn't it?"

"Yes."

"So, check in your computer. Certainly such an important establishment as Shadow Creek Ranch would be listed there."

"That's not possible, ma'am," the man said, glancing at the line of travelers waiting behind the attractive, well-dressed blond, who stood glaring at him from across the counter. "If you'll excuse me, I really must help these other people. We've got a flight leaving for Salt Lake City in 30 minutes."

"I just flew in from there," the woman announced, pointing to the aircraft parked just beyond the large window to their right. "Not a soul on board had ever heard of Shadow Creek Ranch either. What is it with you people? Don't you even know your neighbors?"

"Ma'am, I must insist that you let me help our

other passengers," the clerk pleaded. "It's Christmas Day, and they've got places to go. Perhaps if you check at the information booth over there—"

"Already did. They weren't any help, either." The woman stiffly gathered up her two leather suitcases and fine-sewn garment bag. "How can an entire ranch exist and no one know about it? You people in Montana need to get out more."

With a frustrated sigh, she walked away, ignoring the muffled comments of the passengers who'd been waiting behind her.

Finding a pay phone, she grabbed the phone book and began thumbing through its pages, mumbling as she worked. "Tailors, tanning salons, taverns, tax returns, taxicabs. Here it is— taxicabs!" She laughed out loud. "They've got only one company. Boy, I am in the sticks. But says here, '24-hour service, serving Yellowstone Park, Big Sky, and Livingston'—wherever in the world they are." The woman slipped a coin into the phone and quickly dialed the number. After six rings, a voice answered.

"Bozeman Taxi."

"Yes," the woman called, as if trying to communicate without the phone intervening, "I need a ride from the airport."

"I'm sorry, ma'am, we're closed."

"What do you mean you're closed? Your listing says 24-hour service."

"This is Christmas Day."

"So?"

"So, we're closed on Christmas Day."

The woman's eyes narrowed slightly. "I'll make it worth your while."

The voice on the other end of the line chuckled. "I've got three kids playing with brand-new toys in my living room, a wife baking a pie in the kitchen, and a couple of buddies coming over later to watch the game. That ain't worth all the money in your bank account, lady. I'll be happy to take you wherever you want to go tomorrow, first thing."

"I don't want to go anywhere tomorrow," the woman pleaded. "It's got to be today. I want to be a surprise."

"You surprised the daylights out of me," the man said. "Other than that, I can't help you. Sorry."

"But—"

The line went dead.

"Aaaghhh!" With a resounding thud the woman slammed the phone down on its cradle. "This is a terrible place," she announced. "No one knows where anything is, and those who do don't have the courtesy to take me there. Now what am I supposed to do?"

"Is there a problem, young lady?" a voice called from nearby. The woman looked up to see an older man, dressed in a faded, threadbare work coat, standing by the window. His boots were scuffed, and a red cap sat snugly over his ears.

"Yes, there is," she moaned. "I'm a visitor to your state, and not a soul has lifted a finger to help me."

"Whatcha need?"

"I need to get to a place called Shadow Creek Ranch before the day is over."

"Can't someone from there pick you up?"

"I don't want to call them, because my visit is supposed to be a surprise. They don't even know I'm in this part of the country."

"I see," the old man nodded, rubbing his unshaven face thoughtfully. "You say this place is called Shadow Creek?" He brightened. "I seem to remember hearing about such a ranch south of town 'bout 30 miles. Run by a guy named Hanson."

"Yes. That's it. That's where I want to go."

"Might not be able to get in," the man said. "Snowed last night. Probably closed the road leading into the mountains."

The woman's mouth dropped open. "Don't they plow?"

"Oh sure. But today is—"

"I know. Today is Christmas."

The old man was silent for a moment. "Tell you what. I just put my wife and grandson on the Salt Lake flight. They'll be visiting our son and his wife for the next week. I couldn't go 'cause I gotta work tomorrow. But I might be able to get you to this Shadow Creek Ranch if you'd like. Don't have nothin' else to do today. Could use the company."

"Would you?" the woman gasped. "Could you? I'll be glad to cover your expenses plus a little more."

"Oh, never mind that. Not often a old geezer like me gets to help a pretty lady in distress. Got all your stuff?"

"No. There's an overnight trunk at the baggage carousel. Kind of heavy."

The man nodded. "You get a porter to stack your things by the exit, and I'll go fire up the truck. Be back in 10 minutes."

The blond woman hesitated. "Truck?" Her question went unheard as the old man had already hurried through the front door of the terminal.

As promised he returned, sitting proudly behind the wheel of a large, rattling, vibrating farm truck loaded down with bales of hay and a collection of cut logs. "Helps keep the rear wheels from slipping on the snow," he explained, when he saw his prospective rider eyeing the pile of wood. Jumping down from the cab, he hobbled around to the back of the vehicle, then began tossing her suitcases over the wooden railing above their heads. "We'll just put your bags here by the hay, and you can join me in the cab. Heater works good most the time, 'cept your feet get kinda hot, so you gotta keep the window open a bit. Fresh air never hurt anyone, right?"

The woman adjusted her silk collar and tried to smile.

"This your first visit to Montana?" The man held the door open and motioned toward the torn plastic seat waiting at about his eye level. "You look like you might be from back East."

"Yes, I am," the woman said, trying to figure out how to climb into the cab and still retain a semblance of decorum.

"Just haul yourself up," the man urged, seeing her hesitation. "My wife does it all the time."

"I'm sure she does," she said under her breath. Reaching up she took hold of a cold handrail and gingerly placed an expensive low-cut boot on the high running board. "Now what?" she asked.

"You gotta sorta pull and jump at the same time," he encouraged. "Just swing your free leg up and around. It's really easier than it looks."

The woman grimaced. "I think it's going to be rather awkward."

"Nah. Just do it. I'll help."

"No, that's—"

Strong hands grabbed her legs below the knees, and she found herself being elevated straight up. With a plop she landed in the cab, creating a thin veil of dust with her arrival.

"Perfect!" she heard the man call from somewhere far below. "You'll get the hang of it. Takes a little practice." She watched the top of his head shuffle around the front of the large truck. Then he suddenly appeared at her side, slipping easily into the driver's seat with an amazing degree of grace. "Ignore the smell," he said. "Sometimes we let our German shepherd sit up front with us. He's always

20

digging in things." The man chuckled. "Guess that's what dogs are supposed to do, right?"

"Right."

"So, let's see if we can find your Shadow Creek Ranch. We can ask along the way. People tend to know their neighbors around here."

The woman's head slammed against the seat back as the vehicle lurched forward. "Going to stay in Montana long?" the driver asked.

His passenger tried to speak, but the bouncing cab refused to allow her jaw to operate normally, so she just nodded. With a deep-throated roar and grind of gears, the old farm truck headed away from the airport. Turning onto the southbound highway, it rumbled toward the distant snow-covered mountains.

✻ ✻ ✻

Joey turned the object over and over in his hands, brow furrowed in thought. It was made of wood, that was plain to see. A nail stuck out of it on one end, a white splotch of paint decorated the other, and right in the middle he found his name written in carefully drawn letters. Several holes had been drilled along the top, giving it an annoyingly mysterious appearance.

The boy's lifelong friend, Lizzy Pierce, glanced up from her reading and sat watching him. "Figured it out yet?" she asked.

"No, Dizzy," Joey sighed, tilting his head

slightly and squinting. "I haven't the faintest idea what it's supposed to be."

The old woman chuckled. "Samantha worked long and hard making it, you know."

"I know," the boy nodded. "She was so excited this morning when she gave it to me. Then 'bout an hour ago she'd asked me if I'd *used* it yet. I said I was saving it for later." Joey looked over at his friend pleadingly. "Didn't she say anything to you about what it's supposed to be?"

"Nope. She asked me if I liked Joey's gift, and I said I certainly did. Then she said she'd make one just like it for my birthday."

"Great," the teenager announced. "Then we'll both have one."

Lizzy glanced at the door, then back at Joey. "You could ask her."

The boy shook his head. "It might hurt her feelings."

Just then Wendy strode into the room and plopped herself down in her favorite chair by the big fireplace. She gazed at the flickering yellow flames and stretched tired muscles. "Monty says 'hello' and 'Merry Christmas,'" the girl announced.

"Merry Christmas to Monty," Lizzy responded.

Joey smiled. "How's the ol' pussy cat doin'?"

"Don't call him that," Wendy countered. "He doesn't like it when you call him a pussy cat, because he's far superior to any regular feline on earth."

"Excuse me," Joey laughed. "I forgot how sensitive he is about his name."

Wendy continued staring at the flames. "And he said to thank you again for carrying him out of that cave. Monty thinks you're a hero, although I know different."

Joey winked at Lizzy. "And what exactly do you know about me, Miss Hanson?"

Wendy shrugged. "That you're just Joey Dugan from New York who thinks he can ride horses better than anyone including me, which makes me laugh because Early and I could beat you and Tar Boy any time, 'cept Early can't run right now, so you'll just have to believe me." She glanced at the object in Joey's hands as she rose to leave. "I see you got one too. They work great."

"Wait a minute!" Joey gasped. "You've got one of these?"

"Sure. Sam gave it to me for my last birthday. Just like that one, 'cept mine's green."

"And . . . and you know how to use it?"

"Well, of course! Anybody who doesn't has to be brain-dead."

Joey watched the girl exit the big, cozy den, then looked at Lizzy. "I'm brain-dead," he sighed.

Lizzy laughed. "Maybe you need to think, not as a macho horse-wrangling 17-year-old, but as a first-grader like Sam."

Joey lifted his hand. "Just don't ask me to

think like Wendy. That's not humanly possible."

Lizzy grinned mischievously. "She knows what that gadget is, and you don't."

The boy groaned. "Oh, great. It's Christmas Day, and I find out Wendy's smarter than I am. I'm doomed for life."

Lizzy shook her head. "Don't take it so hard. All you have to do is figure out what Samantha had in mind when she put your gift together. Then you can glory in the thought that you're at least as wise as Wendy."

Joey brightened. "Hold everything! If Wendy's got one of these . . . these things, and knows how to use it, then all I have to do is find hers. Simple." He jumped out of his chair. "I'm a genius."

Lizzy lifted a warning finger. "Be careful," she breathed in hushed tones. "If Wendy finds you sniffing around her stuff, she'll have your hide for supper."

"Not to worry," the boy said confidently. "I'll pay her a visit when she's not in the Station. Then I'll just happen to look around her room by accident, see this whachamacallit in action, and save my pride. She'll never know I was there."

Lizzy's eyebrows rose slightly. "She has ways. Don't ask me to explain them, but she has ways of finding out about the goings on in this Station."

"So do I," the boy said, with more enthusiasm than he truly felt. Wendy could be a formidable foe if crossed. "I'll just use my head, and she'll never catch on. Then I can put this . . . this . . . really great object to work for me. You'll see."

He tucked the gift under his arm and strode from the den, leaving Lizzy shaking her head, a happy grin adding additional wrinkles to her time-worn face.

❄ ❄ ❄

Debbie jumped as she felt a warm kiss planted on the back of her neck. "Barry Gordon," she teased, seeing the smiling, handsome face of the ranch's head wrangler hovering over her, "you scared me to death! Not fair sneaking up on me when I'm trying to wrap your very special, cost-me-an-arm-and-a-leg present."

"What is it?" the young man asked, eyeing the cardboard box half-wrapped with bright paper and resting on the dining room table.

"Now don't go snooping around," Debbie warned, pushing him away. "You'll find out soon enough." She paused. "And speaking of presents, what'd you get me?"

Barry blinked. "Now hold on. How come I'm supposed to tell you what your surprise is, but I can't know anything about mine?"

"'Cause that's the law," the girl stated, rising and squirming herself into his strong arms. "Girls have special privileges. We're different, you know. Unique. We're supposed to be treated with utmost respect and our every wish fulfilled without question."

25

Barry laughed. "I guess the women's movement didn't make too much of a dent in you. But I agree. I don't know about all other beautiful, dark-haired, slender, fashion-conscious women of the world, but you certainly are one unique female-type person. And I especially like your taste in men."

"Is that so?" the girl purred. "I go for the sensitive, mature type with brown hair and blue eyes. If they walk with a cane, so much the better."

Barry grinned. "You like the cane, huh?"

"Yup."

"If I know you, you'll use it to keep *me* in line."

Wendy walked into the dining room, saw the two standing in each other's arms, rolled her eyes, sighed, and exited.

"I think my kid sister approves of us," Debbie smiled.

"How could you tell?" Barry questioned.

"She didn't throw anything."

"Good point."

Debbie wiggled away and placed her hands on her hips. "Now you'd better get out of here so I can finish wrapping your present." She softened. "How was your Christmas morning?"

The wrangler moved toward the door, leaning on his cane. "It was great. Mom and Dad say 'hey' and send their love. They're looking forward to seeing you tomorrow. We can leave right after Joey and I feed the livestock in the morning. Mom's fixin' a chocolate cake and some homemade ice cream for lunch. Be prepared to gain a few pounds."

Debbie grinned. "Your mother would certainly not be welcomed at a Weight Watchers convention."

Barry lifted his palm and blew the girl a gentle kiss. Debbie caught it and pressed it against her lips. "I love you," she mouthed.

"WHAT?" the wrangler called out in a voice loud enough for the whole Station to hear. "Did you say something?"

Debbie reddened and hid her face in her hands as he turned and hurried from the room, his laughter filling the house and her heart with joy.

✲ ✲ ✲

The vibrating cab of the truck lurched to a stop, almost tossing its passenger into the windshield. "There's ol' Harold Kuebler," the driver called out, reaching down and pulling on the emergency brake handle. "He knows everyone in the Gallatin Valley. I'll bet two weeks' pay that he can tell us how to find your Shadow Creek Ranch."

The woman watched as he pushed open his door and dropped from sight. Soon he and Mr. Kuebler were in friendly conversation by a fence row, each gesturing first to the right, then to the left as they outlined and reviewed detailed directions and travel instructions.

After five minutes had passed, the farmer hurried back to the cab, arriving, as before, suddenly and gracefully. "Just as I figured; Harold knows the Hanson clan well. Said they're good, honest, hardworking folk."

"Are we heading in the right direction?" the woman asked, trying to catch a glimpse of herself in the side mirror in anticipation of her arrival.

"Almost," her driver called, jamming the truck into first gear. "Gotta take State 191 a little farther south 'till it crosses the river. Then about five or six miles later we'll see an old, run-down, abandoned barn on the left. Next road after that leads into the mountains and to Shadow Creek Ranch."

"How about the snow on the unplowed road?"

"Harold seems to think we'll be OK. Got a good load of logs back there, you know."

"Yes, you told me."

"Helps with traction."

"Right."

Pulling out onto the main highway again, the farmer shifted gears and glanced at the newly plowed road stretching out ahead. "Pretty country, ain't it?" he said, his words more of a statement than a query.

The woman studied the approaching towering mountains with their white caps and broad, granite shoulders. Pine trees, straight as rulers, rose like green sentries in places no human had ever walked. And then, suddenly, they were among them, as if the land had swallowed them whole.

As he guided his noisy truck along the icy roadway, the farmer grew silent, his friendly chatter fading away. The mountains seemed to have the ability to draw all words, all thoughts, all expression from the mind, leaving only one feeling in their wakes—humbleness.

After a long stillness, he repeated, "Pretty, ain't it?"

The woman nodded. She too had fallen victim to the soul-stirring beauty surrounding them. She had seen nothing like this in the East, nothing that even came close. Her world had been filled with big-city traffic, busy suburbs, and ringing telephones. If she hadn't watched the news on a particular day, she felt lost and uninformed. To her, beauty was always something man-made, something created with big budgets and exotic materials, like the coat she was wearing or the car she drove. But here was loveliness untouched by designers and craftsmen. Here was majesty beyond words that somehow made her feel small and unimportant. She couldn't purchase a mountain. The credit limits on her bankcards were nowhere near enough to cover the cost of just one small valley or wandering stream. For the first time in her life she recognized that she couldn't buy what she found appealing. In this land of earth and sky she could only browse among the priceless vistas and unspeakable joys found at every turn. The thought disturbed her just a little.

"There it is!" an excited voice broke into her reverie. "There's the old barn. Watch for the cutoff."

The woman nodded and leaned forward against her shoulder harness, eyes glued to the left side of the road. Soon they saw a small snow-covered lane angling from the highway, following a narrow valley deeper into the mountains.

"Piece of cake," the driver shouted over the roar of the downshifting engine. "Snow's not bad at all. This old truck won't even know it's there. Hang on, pretty lady, we're headin' for Shadow Creek Ranch."

The woman grabbed hold of the door latch and glove compartment as the truck rumbled onto the snowy roadbed. With a lurch and bump they continued their journey, heading directly into the majestic landscape that sparkled and shone under the late afternoon sun.

❄ ❄ ❄

Samantha's dark face appeared at the doorway of Joey's room, her broad smile framed by small ringlets of hair. "Supper's ready," she called. "Me and Grandma Hanson made cheese sandwiches, a tossed salad with French dressing, lentil soup, and peach ice cream. We also got milk and a few other things that I don't know about."

Joey closed his eyes in ecstacy. "Grandma Hanson's lentil soup. I can taste it now!"

The little girl entered the room and ambled over to the foot of Joey's bed. She looked around. "Where's my gift I gave you?"

The boy cleared his throat. "Well, now, I just haven't put it up yet. Do you think it would look nice on my bed?"

Samantha giggled. "Of course not, silly."

"Of course not," Joey repeated, studying his friend's face carefully. "How 'bout up on the dresser?"

The girl laughed. "Now why would you want to put it up there?"

Joey laughed too. "I'm just being silly."

"Yes you are," Samantha giggled. "You're always silly."

The young wrangler's brow furrowed slightly. "How 'bout the closet? Should I put it in there?"

Samantha almost doubled over with glee. "In the closet? That would be so funny!"

"Yes it would," Joey agreed, his mind whirling. "How 'bout out in the tack house?"

Samantha nodded. "Sure, it would work out there too, 'cept I made it for this room. Didn't you see the color?"

"White. Of course," Joey said, lifting his hands as if to say *What was I thinking?* "The only place it will work best is here in my bedroom, right?"

"Right," the girl stated.

"And exactly where would you think it looked the nicest?"

Samantha burst out laughing again. "Come on, Joey, you're making my tummy hurt with your jokes." She hurried to the door. "You'd better come

31

for supper. The sooner we eat, the sooner I can get to the peach ice cream."

"You're absolutely correct," the boy said, jumping to his feet. "Let's get to the dining room as fast as we can before some big bear comes in and eats our food."

With a happy squeal, Samantha raced down the hallway leading to the front of the Station. Joey glanced around the room, trying with all his might to figure out where his gift was supposed to be placed. Then he gave up in frustration. He'd have to depend on his original plan. Wendy's room held the answer. One way or another, he'd discover the purpose of Samantha's mysterious gift.

The dining room contained its usual collection of cheerful voices and hearty laughter. After all the residents of Shadow Creek Ranch had settled themselves at the long, wooden table, Grandpa Hanson lifted his hand, bringing conversation to an abrupt end. "Let's pray," he said softly. Every head bowed and every eye closed. "Father in heaven," the old man began, "thank You for this delicious meal we're about to enjoy. May we be ever thoughtful of those who aren't so blessed. For Your love and care, we are grateful. In Jesus' name, Amen."

"Amen," the gathering repeated.

Raising his hand, the speaker motioned for everyone to remain still. "What a wonderful Christmas Day this has been," he said warmly. "I want to personally thank every one of you who showered this old man with such delightful, thoughtful gifts. To the one who put a piece of coal in my stocking, may you sleep in a snowdrift for a year." Giggling burst out across the table. "And to whoever it was who sang 'Santa Clause Is Coming to Town' outside our bedroom door at 3:00 this morning, I just want to say you were flat and your rhythm was all wrong."

Grandma Hanson looked up at her husband. "No one sang outside your door last night, old man. You just heard yourself snoring."

Wendy shook her head and pointed at her grandfather. "Was that you? I thought Monty had come down from the mountain and was serenading us."

Grandpa Hanson pouted. "I don't snore Christmas carols. Show tunes, maybe."

"Sit down before our soup evaporates," his wife ordered, pulling at his sleeve. "We'll discuss your nocturnal concerts later." Everyone applauded as the old man slumped into his chair at the head of the table, looking dejected and abused. His wife leaned over and planted a kiss on his cheek. With that Grandpa Hanson sat up straight, glanced around, and said, "What's to eat? I suddenly have a voracious appetite!"

Eager spoons dug into steaming soup bowls as the conversation built back to its normal, cheery level. There was something special about meal-time at Shadow Creek Ranch, but that shouldn't have surprised anyone. The old Station was used to feeling the pulse of joy beating within its broad-beamed rooms and hallways. Hadn't it served travelers for generations before Grandpa Hanson purchased it? Hadn't it welcomed stagecoaches and wagons for years, even to the turn of the century, before modern highways and automobiles provided more convenient access to Yellowstone National Park farther to the south? Within its walls hid endless stories of love and adventure. Deep in its wooden fabric vibrated echoes of excited words spoken by men, women, boys, and girls who'd stayed a night or two amid the mountains and valleys before continuing their journeys to places beyond the horizon. The Station, like the ranch that eventually spread out around it, had always rung with the voices of people who loved the land and the freedom it provided.

This late afternoon gathering was no different. It was in keeping with the history of the place.

As shadows crept across the snow-covered meadows and pastures, dimming the sky to a soft hue, an old farm truck made its way toward the large, two-story structure. Its passenger studied the handsome edifice with the broad front porch and its tall chimneys rising from behind each side. "This is it," she said to her driver. "I know this is it. I'm finally here."

The old man at the wheel stopped his truck and jumped down from the cab, his feet crunching in the snow. He helped her leave her high perch and then carefully handed her the suitcases.

"Gotta head back before it gets completely dark," he said with a smile, his words forming clouds in the frigid air. "Sure is a nice place. Merry Christmas to you, ma'am."

"Thank you," the woman said, taking his hand in hers. "You've been my knight in shining armor today."

The man blushed and hurried back to the cab. "Have a good visit," he called as he flipped the ignition key, causing the engine to roar to life. In seconds he was gone, leaving the woman standing before the Station, bathed in its yellow light, alone in the gathering darkness.

Debbie was just about to take a bite of her peach ice cream when she thought she heard something. Putting down her spoon, she jumped up. "Think there's someone at the door," she called over her shoulder as she headed out of the dining room into the big foyer. "I'll see who it is."

"Probably the Dawsons," her dad suggested, savoring a mouthful of cheese sandwich. "They said they'd try to get down if the high mountain roads weren't too bad. Tell 'em we've got lots of soup left."

The girl arrived at the big front door and swung it open eagerly. "Hi," the woman said.

Debbie stared at her for a long moment, saying nothing.

"Aren't you going to invite me in?" the visitor asked softly.

The girl motioned for her to enter. With a smile, the newcomer lifted two of her suitcases and stepped forward, feeling the warmth of the Station envelop her as she entered the building.

"Where is everybody?" the woman asked, eyeing the two curving staircases arching up to the second-floor balcony.

"In here," Debbie said, pointing toward the dining room.

Wendy had just finished telling a particularly funny story about Early when she glanced at the doorway leading into the hall. Her words froze in her mouth. Conversation ceased as all eyes stared at the woman standing beside Debbie.

Joey looked around. "What's going on?" he asked. "Who's our visitor?"

Slipping from her chair, Wendy slowly moved toward the front of the room. As she approached the woman, she broke into a run and threw herself into outstretched arms.

Joey looked over at Mr. Hanson, who sat motionless by his father, face pale and expressionless. In the stillness the boy heard Wendy speak one word that made his heart stop mid-beat. With a voice not much above a whisper, she cried, "Mother."

CHAPTER 2

Silent Night

"Were you surprised?" the woman asked as Mr. Hanson placed the last of her designer luggage in one of the empty guest rooms. "You looked a bit startled."

"What are you doing here?" came the quick reply.

"Now, that's no way to talk to a visitor at the famous Shadow Creek Ranch," she pouted. "Wendy told me in her letters that you welcome all kinds of strays in from the cold—human and otherwise."

"I don't have time for you," he said.

"You never did."

Mr. Hanson stiffened. "You left our lives years ago, Ellen. We've all gotten used to the idea of not having you around."

"I made a mistake," the woman sighed. "I know that now. I was younger, more vulnerable."

"You've never had a vulnerable day in your life," he shot back. "You knew what you were doing. That . . . that gentleman from Connecticut you ran off with didn't require anything of you. No responsibilities, no kids, no clothes to wash, no bills to pay. Just *love*." Mr. Hanson said the word like it didn't taste good. "I believe that's the way you described the situation to me. A life filled with freedom and joy? Well a man can love a woman in many ways, like working his tail off to provide for her and the kids. Did you ever stop to think that perhaps my love for you was worth more than a fat bank account and a big house in the country?"

"Let's not get into this," Ellen moaned. "It's ancient history."

"Hey, we live with that history every day," the lawyer said. "Me, Debbie, and Wendy."

"Don't you think I do too? Don't you think I remember what I did? I was their mother!"

Mr. Hanson nodded. "That's right, Ellen. You *were*."

Footsteps sounded in the hallway, bringing the conversation to a halt. Wendy's smiling face appeared in the doorway. "This is the best Christmas surprise I've ever had!" she said breathlessly, entering the room with her arms burdened with hastily wrapped gifts. "If I'd known you were coming, I would've spent all my money at the mall getting you stuff. But me and Sam found lots of presents for you in our room. I hope you like them."

Little Samantha stumbled along behind Wendy, almost tripping over her heels. "I got you a pretty rock me and Pueblo found in the creek.

Pueblo's my dog. He lives out in the horse barn with Early and Tar Boy. Sometimes he barks at the moon." She giggled. "Yeah, like the moon's going to attack us or something. He's a strange critter, but he's my friend, and we found this yellow-and-pink rock, and you can have it." She lifted a wrapped object up for the woman to see. "It'll make a great doorstop."

The visitor smiled and took the package from Sam's small hands. "I'm sure it's lovely, Samantha," she said. "Thank you."

"Oh, we got lots of stuff for you!" Wendy broke in, her excitement causing her feet to dance. "You can start with this one, after you open Sam's rock."

Mr. Hanson turned to leave. At the door he glanced back at his ex-wife. She smiled at him, then directed her attention to the gifts now scattered across the bed, and to the joyful faces of the girls chattering about her.

As he walked down the long upstairs hallway he saw Debbie standing at the balcony railing. When he reached her, he slipped an arm around her waist, and they stood together in silence for a few moments.

"It's not fair," the girl finally said softly. "She shouldn't be here."

"I know."

Debbie laid her head against her father's shoulder. "It makes me angry. I didn't want to feel this way ever again."

"I know."

"What does she want, Daddy? What is she trying to prove?"

The man sighed. "She said she made a mistake."

Debbie blinked. "We're supposed to forgive her?
Is that what she wants? We're supposed to say 'It's
all right that you left your family when they needed
you. It's all right that you broke our hearts'?"

Her father ran a hand through his hair. "I don't
know what she's up to. If it was my decision, I'd
put her on the next plane back to Connecticut. But
Wendy's beside herself with joy. She's like a little
girl again, not the rough, tough kid who makes life
miserable for Joey or falls into underground caves
and comes out clutching a mountain lion. It's as if
time has rolled back for her, as if she's picking up
where she left off with Ellen."

Debbie looked into his eyes. "Do you love
me, Daddy?"

The man smiled. "More every day, Debbie.
You're my treasure, you and Wendy. We're a family, and nothing's going to change that." He motioned toward the stairs. "And isn't there a young
man down in the den who's missing you almost as
much as I do when you're away?"

Debbie wrapped her arms around her father.
"Seeing Mom again makes me scared inside. But
when you hold me, I feel better."

"Then you can order up a hug anytime, sweetheart. That's what dads are for."

The girl nodded and started down the stairs. After a few seconds she paused. "Ms. Cadena is coming out tomorrow with the kids," she said. "Maybe we can ask her how to handle this situation."

Mr. Hanson shook his head. "Don't be so obvious," he chuckled.

Debbie grinned, then continued down the steps and hurried into the den.

❆ ❆ ❆

Ruth Cadena stood on one foot, then another, trying to catch a glimpse of the passengers deplaning at the airport. The day-after-Christmas crowd surged through the small terminal still filled with holiday spirit and colorful decorations. But for Ms. Cadena it wasn't a vacation day. She wasn't there to greet family members or long-lost friends. Her task was to gather up four arriving teenagers—three from Chicago, one from Orlando—and shuttle them into the mountains to a ranch called Shadow Creek.

She glanced again at her clipboard. The three Chicago passengers would be about the same age—15—two boys, one girl. She had snapshots of each.

The Orlando girl would be younger—13. They'd all been instructed to look for a tall, slender Hispanic woman, who was wearing a red coat and a matching knit hat resting over shoulder-length dark hair. Just to make sure there'd be no confusion, Ms. Cadena was carrying a small sign

41

that had "Shadow Creek Ranch" written in blue letters across it.

Soon three rather lost-looking young people wandered into the passenger receiving area. The woman lifted the sign high above her head. "Over here," she called, trying to be heard above the happy chatter. "Tucker? Garth? Ashley?"

The new arrivals turned as they heard their names called. Seeing the woman and the sign, they changed direction and started hesitantly across the crowded room.

"Hi, I'm Ruth Cadena from Project Youth Revival," she said, easing the tension immediately with her open, honest smile. "Did you have a good flight?"

The taller of the two boys, Tucker, nodded and glanced around, his blue eyes narrowing slightly. "How far is the ranch from here?"

"Not too far," she assured him. "You're going to love it. Really."

"I don't like mountains," he stated.

"I don't blame you," the woman responded, trying to keep one eye on the passengers still deplaning. "Chicago's rather flat. But these mountains'll grow on you."

"I don't mind them so much," the other boy said with a shrug, adjusting the baseball cap perched atop his dark, smoothly shaven head. "I visited Colorado once. They got lots of mountains."

"Do we have to ride horses?" the girl asked.

"No, Ashley," Ms. Cadena responded, admiring the teenager's smooth skin and light-brown curls. "Not unless you want to."

Suddenly they heard a commotion in the jetway leading out to the airplane. A man's voice shouted something, and the next moment a young, slightly built girl burst through the crowd and hurried by. She was just about to reach the main terminal area when a security guard materialized out of nowhere and grabbed her by the back of the coat. The big Black man planted his feet and brought the running teen to a quick halt.

"Let me go. LET ME GO!" the girl screamed, swinging her arms in the air, trying to reach the guard holding her away from his body.

Glancing down at the photograph fastened to her clipboard, Ms. Cadena sighed. Her fourth charge had arrived.

"She's mine, Billy," the woman called as she and the others hurried over to where the guard stood.

"Well, Ruth Cadena," the man smiled broadly, still holding the swinging child, "you sure know how to pick 'em."

"Don't I though?"

A passenger ran up to the little gathering. "She stole my wallet," he announced, pointing at the squirming girl. "I demand that you put her in jail this minute, or the airline will certainly hear about this."

"You want me to throw this little kid behind

bars?" the security guard asked, lifting the girl up for him to see. "What is she, 5 years old?"

"FIVE!" the prisoner yelped, suddenly ceasing her wild flaylings and hanging limply. "I'm 13 and a half!"

"Where's my wallet?" the passenger demanded.

"Wallet? What wallet?" the girl asked sweetly.

"You know good and well what wallet. You took it out of my back pocket in the jetway. I felt it go."

"You did?" the teen blinked. "Man, I'm losin' my touch."

"Just give it back to me, or you're in big trouble."

Ms. Cadena stepped forward. "Sir, this child is under my supervision here in Montana. If you'll allow me to handle this, I'll get your valuables back in just a second."

"Who are you?" the girl asked.

The youth worker walked over to her and placed her nose inches from hers. "I'm your worst nightmare," she said in low tones. "I'm gonna take you into the mountains and stick you on a horse and send you galloping across high meadows and rocky hilltops. I'm gonna feed you more food than you can hold while you suck in enough fresh air to purify your lungs for a month. Not only that, I'm gonna teach you how to bake bread, read a compass, survive a snowstorm, and maybe, just maybe, I'll let you bring supper to a real, live mountain lion."

The girl blinked, then smiled. "Cool," she said.

"Now," Ms. Cadena continued, "if you'll just give this nice gentleman back his wallet, we can get underway, unless, of course, you wanna fly back to Florida on the next departure."

The young teen lifted her hands. "What do you think I am, a thief?"

"That's exactly what you are," Ms. Cadena stated flatly. "But that's about to change, right?"

The two looked at each other for a moment, then the girl sighed. "OK, OK. Here." She reached into her coat pocket and pulled out a worn, shiny leather wallet. The man grabbed it from her hand and quickly thumbed through its contents. With a huff, he turned and hurried away.

"Sir?" the girl said, addressing the security guard. "Could you put me down now?"

The big man smiled. "With pleasure, little lady." He lowered his burden gently to the floor and winked at Ms. Cadena. "She's all yours."

The woman studied the youngster thoughtfully. "Well, Luisa. Am I going to have any more trouble out of you, or should we take Billy along just in case?"

Luisa grinned sheepishly. "That's OK. I'll behave myself. But that guy was such a jerk on the airplane. He kept buggin' the flight attendants and flirtin' with the lady sitting next to him. He deserved to have his wallet lifted."

Ms. Cadena sighed. She'd heard similar reasoning before. Many young punks believed they were doing the world a favor by harassing others. Luisa had a long history of larceny. That's why she'd spent so much time in and out of detention centers. And that was why she was here.

After quick introductions, Ruth Cadena announced, "OK, you guys, we've gotta get going. We'll stop by baggage claim to collect your stuff, then head out to my van. And don't cause me any more grief. It's the holidays, and I'm in a jovial mood. Don't spoil it."

Her four charges smiled and nodded. There was something about Ruth Cadena they hadn't expected. She was honest, truly open and aboveboard. During their repeated trips through the juvenile justice system they'd met all kinds of people, some more pleasant than others. Here was a woman who seemed almost vulnerable, yet possessed an inner warmth they found irresistible. She looked genuinely glad to see them. It felt good to be the cause of another person's happiness for a change.

As the group headed south out of the airport in the red minivan Ms. Cadena had borrowed from Mr. Hanson, the woman reviewed silently the case studies of each teen. Tucker Williams, the tall, blue-eyed boy sitting across from her, was on probation for dealing drugs. It was his first offense. The authorities were hoping his visit to Montana might direct his interests elsewhere.

Garth Meyer, a Black youth from Chicago's south side, had an arrest record as long as a horse's leg—everything from breaking and entering to suspected arson. His neatly shaved head was an indication he belonged to a particularly rough street gang near his home called the Rip Tigers. But the local juvenile authorities had seen promise in him and contacted Project Youth Revival.

Ashley Hart, the pretty Latino with the Anglo name and the long brown curls, hailed from a small town near Chicago. Her crimes included prostitution and assault. She, like the two boys, was 15.

Then there was Luisa Adams. Ms. Cadena glanced in the rearview mirror and studied the young, cherublike face of her troublesome charge. The girl sat watching the snow-covered fields slip by beyond the frost-ringed window. Luisa hailed from sunny Orlando, Florida, and had a nasty habit of relieving people of their possessions. "She's a firecracker," the police chief had told Ruth over the phone. "But I think she's a good kid under all that bravado. Her home life stinks. She has every reason to be rebellious, yet she's a favorite in our precinct because she has such a terrific sense of humor. We're hoping you can turn her toward more legal hobbies like reading or football or anything. She can run like a scared rabbit."

Ms. Cadena grinned, remembering the officer's words. She'd seen a demonstration of that particular skill 20 minutes ago. At 13, Luisa represented a genuine challenge to the Project Youth Revival program and the good people waiting at Shadow Creek Ranch.

Instantly Ruth suppressed a certain grin before it had a chance to brighten her face. It happened every time she thought of Tyler Hanson, Debbie and Wendy's good-looking father. Funny how he seemed to pop up in her thoughts so often. He'd reported that he was plagued by the same problem, only she was the unexpected guest in his musings. A kind, forgiving man, he was a rare find as far as she was concerned. She gave in and let the happy smile crease her face. He'd be waiting with the others as she drove down the long driveway leading up to the Station. Yes, the day seemed brighter simply because Tyler Hanson was going to be a part of it.

The little red minivan continued along the freshly plowed highway, heading toward the mountains with its load of young teens and a woman determined to influence their lives for the better.

* * *

"They're coming. THEY'RE COMING!" Samantha's energetic voice rang out from her perch by the window fronting the Station's upstairs office.

Mr. Hanson cringed. "Hey, Sam. You're killin' my ears. Shout softer."

The little girl took in a deep breath and whispered in a hoarse voice. "They're coming. They're—"

She paused. "That doesn't work, Mr. Hanson," she announced. "No one can hear me."

The lawyer grinned. "You're right, Sam. Let 'er loose."

With a happy squeal, the dark-skinned favorite of the ranch clan raced from the room and slid down the curving banister leading to the lower level, her voice echoing in every nook and cranny of the old Station. "Get ready, everybody. Our guests have arrived!"

Mr. Hanson glanced out the window to see his minivan plowing through the snow still clinging to the long driveway. He saved the computer file he was working on and switched off the machine. For a moment he sat in the sudden stillness, thinking about the job he and the others faced. A small group of kids who needed love and direction in their lives were about to become part of their ranch family for the next 14 days. As always, he bowed his head and sent a quick prayer heavenward, asking for guidance. He added a short addendum. "Lord, what am I supposed to do about Ellen?"

As Tucker, Garth, Ashley, and Luisa stepped down from the van, they found themselves surrounded by smiling faces and cheerful voices. Introductions were made, hands shook, pleasantries exchanged, then the Shadow Creek Ranch family hastily brought them and their suitcases inside.

Wendy kept watching Luisa to see how she was

49

reacting to the chill air and white, fluffy snow filling the valley. "So, how do you like Montana?" she asked as they plopped the girl's two suitcases and a carry-on bag on her bed.

"It's a little chilly," Luisa responded.

Wendy blinked. "A little chilly? It's 11 degrees outside! Betcha ya don't see 11 degrees too much in Florida."

The newcomer thought for a moment. "Can't say as I have."

Wendy's brow furrowed. "How 'bout the snow?"

Luisa shrugged. "It's like sand, only wetter."

"Wow," the girl gasped. "I thought you'd be amazed or something. Most people, when they see snow and stuff for the first time, can hardly believe their eyes."

"Nothin' surprises me," Luisa said without emotion.

"I guess not," Wendy nodded. Pointing at the baggage, she added, "As soon as you're unpacked, I'll show you the most beautiful horse in all of Gallatin Valley. Name's Early."

"Sure. I'll be out in a minute."

Wendy walked to the door. "I can also introduce you to a real mountain lion."

"Great," the visitor said halfheartedly.

Wendy shook her head slowly as she exited. Luisa was going to be a tough sell. If there was one thing Wendy enjoyed, it was surprising or shocking people. The weather hadn't done it. The prospect of meeting a mountain lion hadn't even raised an eyebrow. What did it take to impress this new girl?

As the door to her bedroom closed, Luisa moved slowly to the window. Ice crystals had formed around the edges, creating a clear, transparent frame filled with intricate, delicate designs. She reached up and ran her finger along the glass, feeling its cold, icy surface.

Lifting the sash, she allowed random snowflakes to blow across her face, feeling their sharp edges against her skin. Carefully, hesitantly, she pushed a finger into the small, white drift that had gathered on the window ledge the night before. Then she raised her hand and felt the granules of ice on her tongue. The girl smiled. It was even better than she'd dreamed it would be.

❄ ❄ ❄

"Quite a bunch," Ms. Cadena said with a smile as she and Mr. Hanson surveyed the group who'd gathered in the den to hear Grandpa Hanson's official welcome. A warm fire crackled in the large stone hearth, illuminating the bookcases, small desks, and comfortable chairs scattered about the broad room with a peaceful yellow light. Soft, evening shadows were fading into night just beyond the large, lace-curtained windows.

The lawyer grinned. "Yes, they are. Did everything go well at the airport?"

Ruth swallowed a little harder than usual.

"Let's just say we got out with no lives lost."

Mr. Hanson glanced over at her. "Something tells me I don't want to know what happened."

She nodded. "Something tells me you're right." The man shook his head and chuckled.

"Aren't you going to introduce me to your friend?" a soft female voice inquired from behind them in the foyer. Mr. Hanson and Ruth turned to find Ellen standing by the staircase, a curious smile on her face.

"Hello," Ms. Cadena said, extending her hand. "I don't believe we've met." She looked over at Mr. Hanson.

The man cleared his throat. "Ruth," he said, "this is . . . is . . . my ex-wife, Ellen."

The youth worker blinked. "Oh," she responded, her hand still poised in front of her. "I didn't know you were coming for winter camp."

The woman reached out and touched Ms. Cadena's fingers, shaking them lightly. "That's not exactly what I came for," she stated, glancing at Mr. Hanson.

"Well," Ruth said, doing her best to maintain a smile, "we can always use extra help when our guests are here. Perhaps you'd like to be a part of our program for the next few days."

"Oh, I'd just be in the way. From what I hear, you've got everything under control. Wendy's told me a lot about you. She said you're very . . . efficient."

Ms. Cadena shrugged. "I usually get the job done."

Ellen motioned toward the den. "Ever run into a kid you couldn't change?"

"We're not here to change anyone," Ruth stated. "We want to show them there can be more to life than drugs and crime. Our goal is to try to fill their minds with beautiful things, worthwhile activities, genuine loving relationships. Then, if they choose to change the direction of their lives later, they've got something to shoot for."

Ellen's eyebrows rose. "Wendy was right. You are efficient. Smart too." She paused. "Some men even find that attractive in a woman, although I could never understand why."

Mr. Hanson stepped forward. "That was uncalled for, Ellen."

Ruth lifted her hand. "It's OK, Tyler. Your ex-wife is right. Many men feel threatened by an aggressive woman. But I am what I am. I suppose I'm too old to change."

The lawyer's voice shook slightly. "You don't have to apologize for what you are, Ruth."

The youth worker shook her head. "Oh, I wasn't apologizing. I was just explaining . . . efficiently."

With a wave she turned and headed into the den. Mr. Hanson held his tongue for as long as he could. When he spoke, his words were as cold as the icicles hanging beyond the windows. "What do you think you're doing, Ellen? Ruth Cadena is an absolute godsend to children everywhere. She has more integrity than a thousand women I know."

"Does that include me?"

"Right at this moment, yes." The lawyer spun around and walked into the den, leaving his ex-wife standing at the base of the stairs.

"Gather round, everyone," Grandpa Hanson summoned, his voice eager and warm. "Just find a spot and fill it. We're long on family and short on ceremony around here."

The new guests and the others settled themselves in comfortable chairs and soft beanbags as conversations eased into silence. Ellen entered the room and leaned against a bookcase, her eyes studying the woman standing beside the speaker.

"I just want to make it official," Grandpa Hanson called out. "Tucker, Garth, Ashley, and Luisa, welcome to Shadow Creek Ranch. We hope the next couple of weeks will be fun for you and that you'll learn a few things about life on a working ranch. This is our first winter camp, so we'll be kinda making this up as we go. You've met Debbie, Wendy, and Samantha. Joey and Wrangler Barry have already given you a quick tour of the barn, where you met a couple of our horses. That beautiful woman sitting over there is my wife, and next to her is our good friend and home-school teacher, Lizzy Pierce." The man pointed in the direction of the bookcase. "We got a surprise visit yesterday from Ellen Peterson, who, at one time, was Ellen Hanson, my son's wife. That's my baby boy over there." Tyler Hanson grinned broadly and waved. "He's a lawyer," the old man continued, "but try to like him anyway."

Everyone laughed.

"And of course you know the one and only Ruth Cadena, who directs the Montana branch of Project Youth Revival, a national organization dedicated to giving kids a second chance at life. Let's give her a big Shadow Creek Ranch show of appreciation."

The room erupted in wild applause and loud whistles as Ruth bowed deeply from the waist, a happy grin creasing her face. Ellen watched the spectacle silently, her hands remaining at her sides. Then, with a glance toward her ex-husband, she left the room.

❊ ❊ ❊

Wendy snuggled under her covers and shivered from excitement. This was the way she always felt at the beginning of a camp on Shadow Creek Ranch. But the surprise visit of her mother had caused her excitement level to leap clear off the scale. She sighed in the darkness. Imagine, now she could show her *in person* all the things that made her life worthwhile—the high meadows beyond Papoose Lake, her horse Early with his brown eyes and white star, Merrilee Dawson, who'd become an almost surrogate mother to her during the past year, and even Monty looking down from the towering rock formation he called home. No longer would she have to depend on pen, paper, or cassette tape to reveal the deepest pleasures of her life. Now she could take the woman's hand in hers and reveal to her, item by item, what she could only describe before.

Add to this the four new visitors, who even now were snug in their own beds about the Station, and life couldn't possibly hold any more excitement.

Wendy listened to the stillness of the large building with its covering of snow and darkness. Little Samantha's steady breathing from across the room soon lulled her to sleep, where soft visions of adventures to come filled her dreams.

The girl wasn't sure what awakened her. It hadn't been the call of a bird as happened so often in the spring. Pueblo hadn't barked, for he was curled up in the horse barn beyond the footbridge. Wendy blinked, her eyelids heavy and dry. Maybe Samantha had coughed. But a few moments of listening suggested the child was still deep in slumber.

Then she heard a sound she'd didn't recognize. It was low, almost lost in the stillness.

Her eyes fluttered open again as she lay on her bed. Moonbeams filtered through the curtains, illuminating in cold, dull light the ceiling fixture and dresser. She could see her nightstand and lamp, her picture of Early on the wall, her favorite riding boots resting by the door. The color had drained out of the room, leaving only shades of silver and grey.

The sound rose again, faded as if something had stirred, then vanished.

Lifting herself up on one elbow, Wendy waited, listening, listening. She heard only a delicate ringing in her ears, a sound she knew was produced by the blood circulating through her veins.

Then it came again, from somewhere seemingly far away.

The girl pushed back the covers and gently lowered her feet into waiting slippers. Moving silently across the room, she lifted her thick, soft bathrobe from the hook on the wall and slipped her arms into the sleeves.

The doorknob felt cold in her palm as she turned it slowly until the door eased open, revealing an empty hallway. Nothing stirred in the shadows.

She stood for a long moment, waiting for the sound to be repeated. Then, just as she was about to admit to herself that her overactive imagination was playing its usual tricks on her, she heard a long, low moan drift in the cool, unmoving air. At that same moment, the tall, regal clock in the den began to chime out the hour. *"Bong . . . bong . . . bong . . ."*

The girl felt herself opening the door wider and taking a hesitant step into the hall.

"Bong . . . bong . . . bong . . ."

The sound was coming from the last door on

the left, a door hidden deep in the dark shadows cast by the long passageway.

"Bong . . . bong . . . bong . . ."

Drawn by the low moan that seemed to penetrate her body and wrap unseen fingers around her heart and lungs, Wendy crept forward.

"Bong . . . bong . . . bong."

It was midnight. As the last strike of the clock faded away, she stood before the door, hands trembling at her side. Beyond it the moaning continued. Suddenly she realized that what she was hearing wasn't just one single sound, but words spoken without rhythm or feeling. It was an endless cadence of mumbled syllables, creating an unearthly groan that seemed to rise from an inhuman voice.

Wendy pressed a hand and ear against the smooth, cold wood of the door, her breathing suspended. It seemed she should be able to understand the words, but she couldn't. They weren't clear enough.

All at once the sound ceased. The girl waited, and waited, but the moan had vanished into the shadows.

Turning slowly, she retraced her steps back to her room and closed the door quietly, leaving the Station to the darkness and to the silence of the night.

CHAPTER 3

Word Power

Joey looked up from his workbench to find four faces framed by the open doorway of the horse barn. "Hey, guys," he called out, laying down his tools and slipping off his tall wooden stool. "You ready for the ride of your life?"

Heads nodded cautiously.

"Now, don't get all stressed out," the young wrangler said, opening the bottom half of the swinging door so his visitors could enter the old but sturdy structure. "This is a sleigh ride, not the Kentucky Derby. But, I must warn you that my horse, Tar Boy, is powerful and fast." A twinkle sparkled in his eye. "No tellin' what he might do when he gets out there on the road headin' into the mountains. He's been kinda cooped up in the barn for the past couple days and is rarin' to do some serious pullin'. So you guys had better hold on tight."

Tucker shook his head. "I ain't afraid of a little ol' horse."

Joey's eyebrows rose. "Neither am I. But Tar Boy isn't all that little, and he's certainly not old. Come, I'll show you."

He led the group around to the side of the barn where his horse waited, securely hitched to a large but delicate-looking sleigh. Tucker gasped when he saw the big, black stallion. "Wait a minute," he said. "*That* monster is going to pull us?"

"Yup," Joey nodded.

Tucker looked at the others. "We're all going to die."

The young wrangler laughed. "No, you're not. I'll be driving. Tar Boy will behave himself. I'll make sure he does."

"That's encouraging," Wendy called as she arrived carrying a wicker basket. "One dumb brute being driven by another."

Joey rolled his eyes. "And good morning to *you*, Miss Hanson. By the way, where were you and your mom during breakfast? We particularly missed your usual mindless banter."

Wendy ignored the jab. "Well, Mr. Dugan, if you must know, we had breakfast way before you even got up. I wanted to show my mom what the valley looks like as the sun rises, so we sat on the overlook."

"On the overlook?" Joey gasped. "What was the temperature up there? Two?"

The girl shrugged. "It was cold, but we didn't care. I told her all about when Debbie and

Wrangler Barry were caught in the snowstorm, and how I fell into the cave. She said I was very brave to find my way out so quickly."

Joey blinked. "Did you tell her how I came down and saved you?"

"I might have mentioned it."

The boy grinned. "That's what I like most about you, Wendy Hanson. You don't leave out any important details."

Wendy fought back a grin of her own. "Oh, don't get all hyper, Mr. Dugan. I said you were like a knight in shining armor, who risked life and limb to save me from a fate worse than death."

"That's more like it," Joey nodded.

Luisa stepped forward. "Did Joey really rescue you from a cave?"

Wendy kicked at a snow clod. "I suppose. But don't get all mushy about it, or that big head of his will get even bigger."

"No chance of that," Joey chuckled. "Not with Wendy around."

Garth pointed at the sleigh. "Where are we supposed to sit on that thing?"

Joey glanced at Wendy and shook his head. Any discussion of his bravery would have to wait. They had a job to do, and the morning was slipping away. With a sigh, he began assigning places for everyone to settle into for the ride.

Soon the valley rang with the happy shouts of teenagers heading out on their very first tour of

Shadow Creek Ranch and the beauties beyond. Tar Boy's powerful legs and shoulders strained against the leather hitch.

The bright sun shown down through the snow-laden arms of the trees, sprinkling the drifts with random patterns of white and shades of gray. Soon all conversation ceased as the passengers found themselves captivated by the unspeakable loveliness of the land. Higher, higher, higher they rode into the mountains, following long-abandoned logging roads. After an hour had passed they crested a rise and found themselves looking far to the horizon.

"That's Mount Blackmore," Wendy announced, pointing to the east. "It's ten thousand, one hundred and ninety-six feet high, which isn't a whole lot compared to other mountains in Montana, but I wouldn't want to fall off it."

"Wow," Ashley breathed. "The highest thing we have in Chicago is the Sears Tower."

"I wouldn't want to fall off that, either," Garth said, squinting into the brilliance of the snow-covered landscape.

Luisa sighed. "The highest thing we have in Florida is taxes." Everyone looked at her. "That's what my dad keeps saying," she said with a grin.

Joey laughed. "I get it. Hey, your father's a funny guy."

The girl shrugged. "Yeah, he's a regular comic."

Wendy leaned forward in her seat. "What's he

like, your dad? Mine's about the weirdest person on the planet."

Luisa glanced away. "How come there are no trees on Mount Blackmore?"

Joey's brow furrowed slightly. "Well, uh, because trees grow only below certain elevations. Ol' Blackmore there is above what's called the timberline. Only little shrubs and bushes can live that high up."

The girl from Orlando nodded and studied the distant horizon. Wendy looked at Joey and shrugged.

"Anybody hungry?" the young wrangler asked, breaking the silence. "Grandma Hanson packed us a—what'd she call it?—a pick-me-up and bring-me-home snack. That was it. Lots of fruit and a bunch of frozen chocolate-chip cookies. Any takers?"

"Yeah!" the group responded eagerly as Wendy fished around under her blanket-covered legs for the basket her grandmother had prepared earlier. They sat on their top-of-the-world perch and enjoyed the summer tastes of apples and pears as they gazed eastward at the majestic march of mountains.

Wendy studied the girl on the front bench beside Joey. Why had she changed the subject so quickly? But more importantly, what was that sound she had heard last night coming from her room? Yes, it was Luisa's room. No question about it—last one on the left at the end of the hall.

Now she had two mysteries to solve instead of

one. And solve them she would. After all, she was Wendy Hanson, a girl dedicated to explaining all the unexplainable in the world.

❅ ❅ ❅

"You and Grandpa hate me, don't you?"

Grandma Hanson looked up from her big pot of stew and saw Ellen standing in the doorway. "No, dear. We don't hate you."

"I had to get away from my life in New York. If you knew what I was going through, you'd understand."

The old woman tossed a pinch of salt into the aromatic, bubbling mixture. "I learned a long time ago to leave the affairs of others alone. I can't possibly know their thoughts, so I don't judge." She looked over at her former daughter-in-law. "You did what you felt you had to do."

"So you agree that—"

"No," the old woman cut her off sharply. "I don't agree with what you did. I only refuse to judge your actions. It's not my place. That's between you and God."

Ellen sat down on one of the wooden bar stools fronting the large work table occupying the middle of the room. Above her scrubbed and shiny pots and pans hung from a metal frame. "You have no idea what it's like to feel the walls closing in on you, to feel trapped. I love Debbie and Wendy. I love Tyler too. It was just . . . just too much for me to handle.

I wanted more than vacuum cleaners and automatic dishwashers. More than afternoon soaps and grocery shopping." She paused. "I had to know that I was worth something. Do you understand?"

Grandma Hanson continued to stir the stew. "And did you find what you were looking for?" she asked. "Did your Mr. Peterson give you what you wanted?"

Ellen nodded. "Yeah. He did."

"And?"

"And . . . it wasn't enough."

The older woman stopped stirring and stared out the window for a long moment. "Tell me something, Ellen. Just what is it you need so badly? What is it that would make you happy?"

She heard her companion sigh. "Since leaving New York, I discovered exactly what I need," the woman said softly. "I need Tyler, and Debbie, and Wendy. I need my family back."

Grandma Hanson turned. "Isn't it a little late for that?"

Ellen's chin lifted as she stared at the older woman. "Perhaps not. I think Tyler still has feelings for me. I know Wendy does. Maybe Debbie too."

"Listen, Ellen," Grandma Hanson said softly, trying to control her emotions. "What you did devastated my son and those girls. Sure Tyler worked too hard. Sure he wasn't as sensitive to your needs as he should've been. I don't blame you for being upset and wanting more in the way of a fulfilling life. But you broke up a marriage. You broke up a family, and that's not an easy breach to repair. Besides, who's to say you'd be happy if you succeeded in pulling it off. Those walls still exist. Home life hasn't changed all that much."

"I've changed," the woman said.

"And so has Tyler. Debbie and Wendy, too. They're not the same people you turned your back on in New York. Each one of them is a little older, and a little wiser."

"It's this Ruth Cadena person, isn't it?" Ellen shot back. "She's trying to take Tyler away from me."

"How can you say that? She doesn't even know you."

"I've seen the way she looks at him."

"A lot of women look at my son," Grandma Hanson said. "He's a kind and honest man. Those are attractive traits."

Ellen stood and clinched her fists. "We'll see who wins. We'll just see!" With that, she turned and walked quickly from the kitchen.

❊ ❊ ❊

Ms. Cadena was waiting for the sleigh as it slid to a stop by the barn. "Did you have a good time?" she called, a smile lighting her friendly face.

Tucker stepped down and brushed snow from his coat. "Yeah, 'cept Joey tried to kill us by racing down the mountain like a crazy person."

"He wasn't trying to kill anybody," Garth laughed, adjusting his baseball cap. "He was just showin' us how fast Tar Boy could run. It was epic."

Ashley nodded her agreement, fingers exploring the front of her face. "We went so fast I think I froze my nose."

"How 'bout you, Luisa?" Ruth called, seeing the passenger sitting beside Joey. "Did you survive the ride?"

The girl shrugged slightly. "Sure," she said.

Wendy landed with a muffled plop beside Ms. Cadena. "Early can run faster. But for an old nag, Tar Boy was OK."

Joey shook his head and winked at Ms. Cadena. "You'll have to excuse Wendy. She musta frozen her senses this morning on the overlook with her mom."

Ruth glanced down at her. "So you and your mother went exploring this morning?"

"Yeah," the girl stated. "She and I have a lot to talk about."

"I'm sure you do," Ms. Cadena agreed. "It must be nice to have her here for a visit."

Wendy slipped a glove from her hand and rubbed her nose with her index finger. "Maybe she'll stay around for a while," the girl suggested. "She says she really likes Montana and thinks she could live on a ranch and everything." The girl looked up at Ruth, her eyes not quite making contact with the woman's. "She *is* my mom, you know."

"I know."

"People make mistakes."

"Yes, they do."

Wendy thrust her hand back into her glove. "Did Grandma say lunch is about ready? I'm starved!"

"Yup," Ruth responded. "Vegetable stew. A Hanson specialty."

Joey closed his eyes in sudden ecstacy. "Hey, guys. You're about to taste the best stew in all of this part of the universe. You all head on in, and I'll unhitch Tar Boy and join you soon. Be sure to save me some."

The group quickly departed, leaving Joey with his work. As he was slipping the harness over his horse's head, he heard someone speak. "Did you really save Wendy from a cave?"

He turned to see Luisa standing by the fence. "Well, it was a joint venture. Me, Mr. Hanson, some park rangers, Wrangler Barry, and a pilot named Hawk. But, yeah, I was the one who went down after her."

"Was it dangerous?"

"You could say that."

The girl thought for a moment. "Why? Why did you do it?"

Joey tilted his head and studied the girl thoughtfully. "Because she's Wendy. I care about her."

"But," Luisa countered, "she says mean things to you all the time."

The young wrangler chuckled. "That's just what Wendy does. She doesn't mean any harm by it."

"How do you know?"

Joey turned and faced the girl, leather reins dangling from his gloved hands. "Well, because . . . because, she just likes to get on my case all the time. I've gotten used to it."

"Does she hit you?"

The wrangler's smile faded. "No. Wendy doesn't hit me. We don't punch at each other around here. Maybe in play, but not seriously."

Luisa nodded, then turned and walked in the direction of the footbridge. Joey stood watching her go, unsure of what to make of their conversation. Something in the girl's questions unnerved him. Maybe it was the look in her eyes, or the tone of her voice. But something wasn't right.

The young wrangler reached up and patted Tar Boy's thick neck. For now he'd better get his chores out of the way. Grandma Hanson's vegetable stew waited at the end of his labors, so he quickly gathered up the harness and carried it into the barn.

❋ ❋ ❋

The afternoon hours flew by as busy afternoons usually do. Luisa and the others received their work assignments for the remaining week, and each took to their duties without complaint. "The first step in becoming worthwhile is to do something worthwhile, and do it well," Ms. Cadena had counseled the teenagers after lunch dishes had been cleared, scrubbed, and put away.

At first Tucker had resisted getting involved with "women's work" as he put it, but when he saw how much fun everyone was having in the kitchen, he decided to join in.

Garth and Ashley got into an argument over which was the best way to clean a pot, Garth insisting that soaking it for at least two days would make the job much easier.

Luisa went about her tasks quietly and carefully. Grandma Hanson decided that she knew her way around a kitchen and spoke approvingly of her work.

After everyone else had left for the den, the old woman stayed behind to help the girl dry the last of the bowls before placing them in the cupboard. "You obviously help out at mealtimes at home," she told her. "Your mother must be taking advantage of your talents."

"My mother is a drunk who spends most of our mealtimes passed out in her own vomit in the living room."

Grandma Hanson gasped. About to scold, she suddenly realized that the girl companion wasn't trying to be crude. She was only being truthful.

"But I clean her up," Luisa continued. "The smell's the worst part. Kinda gets on your skin." The old woman watched the girl carefully wipe a serving bowl. "She doesn't mean to do it. She always apologizes later." Luisa paused. "My dad calls her a worthless tramp, but I know better. When she's not drinking, she cares for me, and cleans up my messes."

Grandma Hanson studied the girl closely. "And your dad?" Luisa slowly folded her dish towel and laid it on the counter. "My dad is a monster," she said. With that, she turned and left the kitchen.

✳ ✳ ✳

Joey stood outside of Wendy's room trying to look casual. It was rare for him to be in the upstairs section of the big Station's south wing, but desperate times called for desperate measures. Just that afternoon Samantha had asked him again if he was "using" her gift.

"I'm still saving it for a special occasion," he reassured his diminutive friend.

Samantha had giggled as if to say, "You're funny, Joey. You don't have to wait. Start using it now!"

He would have been glad to oblige if he could just figure out the purpose of the strange object. He'd even placed it in different spots around his winter bedroom downstairs. But nothing gave him any ideas of what the gift was for. At this moment he knew Wendy was out in the barn with her mother, giving Early his supper. Feeding the livestock was officially his job, but Wendy insisted that, whenever she was on the ranch, she would give her horse his "proper" food, whatever that meant. She used the same oats, hay, and meal he did, but somehow, when she did it, the food transformed into a much more nutritious mixture, capable of creating greater health and vitality. At least, that's what she told everyone.

Glancing first one way, then another, Joey cracked open the door and peeked inside. "Hello?" he called. No response.

Quickly he slipped inside, closing the door.

Wendy and Samantha's room was neat and clean, with everything placed just so. The boy shook his head. For the wild and crazy girl Wendy always seemed to be, she sure was one tidy critter. Pictures of horses, mostly Early, and mostly taken by the animal's owner, lined the walls. Lace curtains, looking out of place in such a rough and sturdy room, hung limp over the closed window, filtering the late-afternoon light.

On the stand next to Wendy's bed rested a framed picture of a much younger Wendy Hanson and her mother, sitting on a couch, laughing. Because of its position, the boy realized that it was the first thing Wendy would see when she awoke in the morning, and the last object she'd notice as she drifted off to sleep. He studied the photograph for a moment, lost in the long-ago fragment of time captured on film.

But gazing at photographs wasn't his mission just now. He had to find out how Wendy was using her gift from Samantha. Joey looked on the dresser, under the bed, on the nightstand, the desk, in the closet, on the window ledge. Nothing.

As he was quietly closing the closet door, Samantha burst into the room, startling him so he slammed his head against the door frame.

"Hi, Joey," the girl called, heading to her desk by the far wall, carrying a brick and an orange. "Why are you hitting your head against the closet?"

The young wrangler thought fast. "Oh, I'm just testing it. Gotta make sure it's strong, you know."

"Why don't you use a hammer?"

Joey gasped. "Why, that's a great idea! I'll go get one. Samantha, you're a genius."

"I know," the girl shrugged, placing her load on the desk and plopping down in her chair.

The boy paused at the door. "Whatcha up to?" he asked.

Samantha studied the objects she'd carried in. "I'm trying to figure out a quicker way of making orange juice."

Joey hesitated, then quickly lifted his hands. "I'll be going now, Sam," he said, backing out of the room. "Don't start your experiment until I'm downstairs, OK?"

"OK," the girl mumbled, lost in thought.

❊ ❊ ❊

". . . and the doctor said in six months to a year, he should be as good as new." Wendy's face shone as the words steamed from her lips in the cold air.

She and her mother were returning from the horse barn and had paused at the footbridge to watch the last rays of the setting sun highlight the clouds building over the distant mountaintops. The air was growing even colder.

"That's wonderful, sweetheart," Ellen said. "But I believe your expert care is helping the animal too. He loves you, I can tell."

Wendy looked into her mother's face and studied her soft blue eyes and the wisps of golden hair jutting from her warm parka. "Mom," she said, "are you and Dad going to . . . to get back together again? Is that why you're here?"

The woman smiled. "Would you like that?"

"Would I! It's like my most important dream. But . . ."

"But what, sweetheart?"

Wendy searched for words. "But how would we know—how would I know that you won't leave us again?"

Ellen bit her lip and turned away as tears stung her eyes.

"Mom," Wendy gasped. "I didn't mean to make you cry. Honest!"

"I know, Wendy. I just feel so bad about what I did to you and Debbie, and to your father."

Small, strong arms encircled her waist. "I missed you, Mom," Wendy breathed, her voice breaking. "But Dad said you'd be happier with that man in Connecticut. So I figured that's where you should be. But I missed you so much."

Ellen dropped to her knees in the snow and grabbed the girl, pressing her close. "I'm sorry, Wendy, I'm so sorry," she cried, tears staining her cheeks. "Please forgive me. Oh, please."

"I forgive you, Mom," Wendy said between sobs of her own. "I really do. You've come back. Now we can be a family again, just like before. Now we can go riding in the mountains in the spring and watch the sunrise from the lookout every day if we want. I can take new pictures of you and me and put them beside my bed. I won't have to write letters 'cause I can just talk to you in person, even if it's 3:00 in the afternoon. Oh Mom, I love you. I love you so much!"

The woman held her young daughter close, rocking back and forth as night crept in around them. Her tears ran uncontrolled, leaving cold reminders of their passing on her face. She glanced over at the Station, its grand exterior looming out of the gathering darkness. Upstairs, where she knew Mr. Hanson's office was located, she could see light and shadows dancing on the inside walls as the man she'd rejected finished up his work for the day. Was there any love for her left in his heart? Could she make Wendy's dreams, and her own, come true?

❊ ❊ ❊

Ms. Cadena knocked lightly on Luisa's door and waited for a response. She was making her nightly rounds, checking that each teen was safely tucked into bed. It was her favorite time of the day, offering her a chance to see how the young people were responding to the experience of living on a working ranch.

"Yes, Mother," she heard a young voice call from behind the portal. The woman smiled and pushed open the door. "So you think I'm being maternal, huh?" she chuckled when she saw Luisa sitting cross-legged on her bed, book by her side.

"Kinda," came the reply.

"Well, your mom's not here, so I get to do the honors."

Luisa grinned. "You're too sober to be related to me."

Ruth sat down beside her. "So, how'd you like your first full day on Shadow Creek Ranch?"

The girl shrugged. "It's OK. I'm havin' fun and everything. Kinda cold, though."

"Yeah. Montana gets this way in late December."

Luisa sighed. "Where'd you live when you were younger?"

"Mexico. Near Mexico City as a matter of fact."

The girl nodded, then pursed her lips. "But there's something strange about the people here."

"Oh?"

"Yeah. They're nice and all, but . . . take Wendy. She's always dumpin' on that horse guy Joey, yet he just lets her do it and laughs it off like it doesn't mean anything."

"He doesn't take her joking seriously, I suppose," the woman said.

"But why doesn't he get hurt, or mad?"

Ms. Cadena leaned forward. "Words can be very powerful things, Luisa," she stated. "They can build or they can destroy. But there's something you've got to keep in mind. Words get their power from us, especially when they're aimed in our direction."

"What do you mean?"

The youth worker thought for a minute. "When someone says something hurtful, and we know this person really means it, we can allow the words to damage us, or we can choose to let them fall harmless at our feet. What Wendy and Joey do is just teasing. They both know it, so they choose not to be permanently affected by the words they say to each other."

Luisa shifted her position. "But what if the other person isn't teasing? What if you know he means them?"

Ruth studied the girl's face. "You can still choose to not let them damage you. It's not always easy, but it's possible."

The girl frowned. "Why do some people say mean things and you know they aren't just kiddin' around?"

"Because *they* haven't learned how to control the power of their words," Ms. Cadena said softly. "They need help. We should pity them."

Luisa shook her head. "No. We should hate them."

"If we do," the woman said, "then we're allowing them to control our feelings, and that's very dangerous."

Luisa sighed and glanced over at Ruth Cadena. "I'm kinda tired, Ms. Cadena. I'd like to go to sleep now."

The woman smiled. "Happy dreams," she said, standing. "We've got neat stuff planned for tomorrow. Wendy's promised to introduce us to Monty."

"Who's Monty?"

Ms. Cadena smiled. "He's a real cool cat."

Luisa giggled. "You mean the mountain lion, don't you? Ms. Cadena, your jokes are, like, really old-fashioned."

The woman turned as she reached the door. "Gotta stop hanging out with Grandpa Hanson. That *cool cat* description was his idea."

With a wave, Ruth slipped out of the room, closing the door behind her.

※ ※ ※

The Station stood stark and alone in the night, a tiny island of life rising from a carpet of dull gray. The moon seemed to drift in the sky, playing hide-and-seek behind formless clouds, spilling its light occasionally on quiet meadows and forested hillsides.

Wendy awoke, unsure of what had called her

out of slumber. Then she knew. The sound had returned, accompanied by the distant chiming of the clock in the den.

This time she hurried along the hallway and positioned herself in the shadows just outside Luisa's room, ear pressed tightly against the door.

The moan came as before, a rambling collection of syllables, void of any rhythm or emotion. She listened, holding her breath, trying to catch the meaning of at least something.

Suddenly the door swung inward, causing the girl to jump. With an erie, almost humanlike screech, it opened, slowly, steadily, until 10 or 11 inches of space gaped between jam and door.

The moan was now clearer, more distinct. Wendy eased into the opening, driven by a mixture of fear and fascination.

The room was dark, tomblike. She could see the dim outline of the bed. Beyond that, the window stood like a phantom, unmoving, its tall panes of glass allowing the soft glow of the snow in the pasture to filter in.

From the inky void of the bed, the moan continued to rise. "No . . . no . . . no . . . plea . . . plea . . ."

Wendy held her breath, listening.

"I not I not I not stop stop stop stop please please sar sar sar no no no no." The moon moved from behind a cloud and cast its light down on the Station. As Wendy watched, the room brightened with a silvery glow, revealing a figure sitting upright on the bed, eyes open, staring straight ahead. Frightened, Wendy held on to the door, unable to run, unable to move.

"Oh oh oh oh sta sta sta stop stop stop I I I I I I hur hur hur hurt hurt hurt hurt hurt—"

Abruptly the moaning ceased and the girl on the bed slumped forward until she lay bent across the blankets. Moonlight shone on her ruffled hair and nightclothes. As she slipped further forward, the uncovered skin on her back began to catch the light spilling in through the window. Wendy's hand shot to her mouth, stifling a gasp. The girl's back was a jumbled mass of dark bruises and raised scars, forming a grotesque map of inter-secting valleys and ridges. Wendy's scream pressed against her palm as her eyes stared at the sight. Suddenly she felt sick and dizzy.

A dark shape brushed past her and moved to the bed. She watched as Ms. Cadena gently lifted and turned the girl until she was lying flat on the sheets. Carefully the woman adjusted Luisa's nightclothes, hiding the scars behind soft folds of flannel. Reaching down, she brought the covers and blankets up to the sleeping girl's chin and then, with utmost care, bent and kissed the teen's flushed cheek, leaving one of her own tears on the pillow beside the ruffled hair.

Turning, Ruth walked to where Wendy stood. "She'll be OK," the woman whispered. "You'd better go back to bed."

Wendy looked up at her in disbelief. "Who?" she gasped. "Who did that to her?"

"Go to bed," Ruth Cadena repeated softly. "We'll talk about it later."

Wendy stared at the sleeping form now safely back under the covers. "Luisa," she whispered, "I'm sorry. I'm sorry."

Ms. Cadena led the girl out into the hallway and guided her back to her room. At the door, Wendy paused. "Can we help her? Can we?"

Ruth sighed and looked down the long hallway. "I hope so, Wendy," she whispered. "I certainly hope so."

With that she vanished back into the shadows from where she'd come. Wendy heard her bedroom door close softly.

For a long moment the girl stood at the entrance to her own room, staring in the direction of Luisa's door, her heart aching. She knew what it was like to be in pain. But she also understood that this was different. This hurt had not been the result of an accident. The pain Luisa lived with wasn't something that could heal after a few visits to a doctor. From what she saw, she knew her new friend had been living a life of constant agony.

Closing her bedroom door, Wendy slipped back between the sheets. Turning, she buried her face in her pillow and cried, her own muffled moan drifting in the midnight air.

CHAPTER 4

Scream

The sun had barely risen above the distant mountain ridges before the Station was buzzing with activity. Although the regular inhabitants of Shadow Creek Ranch were used to getting up with the dawn, their four guests weren't quite as eager to leave dreamland and enter reality at such an early hour. But enticing odors drifting from the downstairs kitchen served to help the newcomers make the transition, stimulating sleepy bodies and minds into action.

Debbie and Wrangler Barry had returned the night before from their two-day visit to the Gordon ranch some miles away where they'd spent a pleasant time visiting Barry's family. For Debbie, Christmas vacation was over. Her task, as always, was to oversee the nature activities of the camp, including the upcoming trip into the mountains to visit Monty.

"It's gonna to be cold up there," she warned as

she joined her charges at the breakfast table. "Dress warmly, with lots of layers to hold in body heat. Oh, and you'll each have your own horse on this outing."

Tucker almost choked on his oatmeal. "What?" he called out, trying to suppress a cough. "Aren't we going to learn how to ride the horses before we head for the hills?"

"We'll teach you on the way," the girl said with a smile. "Wrangler Barry and Joey'll make sure you don't get into any trouble."

Garth sat back in his chair, an excited grin lighting his dark face. "I want to ride the big black one. What was his name? War Bird?"

"Tar Boy," Joey chuckled, spreading grape preserves on a hot piece of toast. "But I'm afraid he's already taken—by me. Don't worry, we'll find you a tough enough critter. I was thinkin' you and Showboat would make a nice team."

"Showboat?" Garth said. "Isn't that the horse that looks like a dalmatian?"

Joey nodded. "Yeah, I guess you can say that. She's an appaloosa—all white with tons of black splotches from head to hoof."

"She?" the boy gasped. "I'm supposed to ride a girl horse?"

Ashley snickered. "Why, Garth Meyer, don't tell me you're scared of a little ol' filly."

Garth grinned. "I'm afraid of anything, male or female, that can throw me off a mountain without even raising a sweat."

Luisa poured cream over her steaming bowl of oatmeal. "Well, if it's OK with everyone, I'm going to ride in the sleigh with Debbie and Wrangler Barry. You guys can play cowboy all you want. I'll be just as happy to wrap up in a blanket and let someone else do the driving."

"Fair enough," Joey nodded.

"May I go too?" a voice called from the doorway. Ellen entered the room and headed for the unoccupied chair beside Wendy.

"Sure," Joey called. "Horse or sleigh?"

"Sleigh, by all means," the woman gasped, seating herself. "I'm not the saddle and whip type." She glanced at the far end of the table. "Well, hello, Debbie. Glad to see you and your friend made it back safe and sound. Did you have a good time?"

The girl reached for the fruit bowl. "Are you still here, Mother?"

"Of course I am. Why shouldn't I be?"

"Oh, I don't know. I'm never sure just how long you'll stay in one spot."

"Debbie!" Mr. Hanson warned, lifting his hand. "This isn't the time or the place."

The girl nodded. "I'm sorry. Yes, Mother. We had a very nice visit. Thanks for asking."

Ellen managed to smile and looked about the room. "So, we're going to meet the famous Monty today, huh? I can hardly wait!"

Wendy grinned broadly. "You'll like him,

Mom," she said. "But don't expect him to be all friendly and stuff. He's still hurtin' kinda bad. His body's really messed up." Luisa's spoon paused midway between her bowl and mouth. "Sometimes he limps and whimpers a little," Wendy continued. "But you should've seen him in the cave. It was awful." The girl's voice faltered as she reached for her half-eaten piece of buttered toast. "I'm going to make him well again. I promised him I would."

"How?" Luisa said softly. "How are you going to make him well?"

Wendy glanced across the table at her. Suddenly, it seemed they weren't in the Station eating breakfast anymore, but were deep underground, in the cave. This time it wasn't a young mountain lion standing just beyond the firelight. Instead, she saw a young girl who'd been battered and bruised, whose nightly cries still echoed in her thoughts. "I'm going to bring him food and talk to him," Wendy said slowly. "I'm going to make sure that he knows I'm his friend and that I'm going to help him any way I can."

Luisa looked down at her oatmeal. "Monty's lucky," she said.

Ruth Cadena cleared her throat, breaking the uneasy silence. "Well, I'm sure everyone can hardly wait to meet Wendy's furry friend. You'd better get this delicious meal stored in your stomachs so you can head for the mountains. Whadda ya say?"

Heads nodded as eager hands grabbed spoons and forks. Happy chatter filled the room again as the sun continued to rise in the east.

❋ ❋ ❋

"Now, just relax and let your horses do all the work," Wrangler Barry called from his perch high on the sleigh. He studied the line of riders, three of whom were sitting rather stiffly in their saddles. "Joey'll bring up the rear. Tucker, Garth, and Ashley, you stay behind me. Wendy and Early will ride point, because they know the way. Is everyone ready?"

"Ready," came the somewhat hesitant reply. Joey chuckled and shifted his position atop Tar Boy. "Will you guys stop worrying? Even if you fall off, you'll land in a nice, soft snowbank."

Ashley shivered slightly. "Isn't there a taxi or something we can hail?"

"Taxi's are for sissies," Garth chided, adjusting his grip on Showboat's reins.

"Yeah," Tucker called, his lanky frame draped over a handsome quarter horse. "Give me the wide open spaces. Give me a star to guide my way. Give me lots of life insurance."

Barry laughed. "Give me a break," he called. "If you guys are finished chitchatting, let's get out of here before the horses drop from sheer boredom."

Wendy lifted her gloved hand. Glancing at her mother sitting bundled in the sleigh, she ordered, "Wa . . . gons, ho!"

"We don't have any wagons," Joey replied as the line began moving forward.

"Use your imagination," Wendy responded over her shoulder.

Soon the horses, riders, and the sleigh carrying Wrangler Barry, Debbie, Ellen, and Luisa headed out across the smooth snow carpeting the valley. Wendy sat straight and proud atop Early, her fondest dream coming true. She knew her mother was watching as she led the caravan into the mountains. The young girl could feel the woman's proud gaze on her back as she maneuvered her horse along the old logging road. It was what she'd missed most—having a mother to watch her grow up.

The new riders quickly discovered that their horses were strong and surefooted, plowing through drifts and passing over slippery spots without a concern. They began to relax and enjoy the natural beauty of the journey.

Joey kept a careful eye on the line ahead, checking to make sure all booted feet stayed in stirrups and hands gripped reins without sending confusing signals to the horses.

The terrain began to rise and in seconds they entered the forest.

❊ ❊ ❊

Monty sat surveying the meadow deep in thought. He was hungry, that was for sure. But what was he supposed to do? He'd seen an occasional mouse scurry past below and had sensed the odor of food many times in the night. But he couldn't run and follow the trail or a scent because his hind legs hurt too much. A fast walk was all he could muster. He knew that a mountain lion couldn't hope to catch anything with a fast walk. Take away the ability to run and pounce, and what do you have? A hungry cat.

It was these and other notions that were running through the big animal's brain when he saw movement at the far end of the meadow. Instinctively, he crouched behind the rocks and waited.

Wendy and Early emerged from the tree line and waded out into the smooth snow of the high-altitude field, the sleigh and the other riders following them into the clearing. The girl eyed the towering rock formation, trying to catch a glimpse of her illusive friend.

"Everybody stay here," she called as Barry pulled on the reins, bringing his sleigh to a halt. Joey and the others rode up beside Wendy. "Do you see him?" the young wrangler asked, patting Tar Boy's neck and studying the distant outcropping.

"Not yet," Wendy stated, "but he's kinda shy. We gotta park our horses back in the forest. Monty gets nervous around them."

"The feeling seems to be mutual," Joey agreed, as Tar Boy began lowering and lifting his head as if saying yes to an unspoken question. The other animals started milling about, snorting softly, causing their riders to tighten the reins.

Suddenly, a scream unlike anything Joey and the visitors had ever heard shattered the cold air. Wendy spun her horse around and shouted, "No, Monty. Don't do that!" But another bone-chilling shriek from the rocks at the far end of the meadow answered her.

Showboat reared up on powerful legs and pawed the air, Garth holding on with all his might. Then, as if catapulted from an aircraft carrier, the appaloosa surged forward, streaking past Joey and the others like a cold rush of air.

Joey dug his heals into Tar Boy's flanks and aimed his mount in the direction of the runaway mare. "Go!" the young wrangler shouted. The stallion responded immediately by lunging forward, hooves digging into the snow.

Wrangler Barry quickly guided the sleigh back into the woods, his companions following close behind.

Garth felt the wind shrieking by as he bent flat against the back of the pitching, rolling animal. Showboat's neck lunged forward and backward inches from his nose. "I'm going to die. I'm going to die!" he kept saying again and again.

He tried to remember what he'd been taught earlier that day. Heels down, knees in, keep low, relax. RELAX! He was hanging onto a spooked horse in a strange meadow high in the Montana mountains, heading straight for a rock formation where a large mountain lion waited, and he was supposed to relax?

Then he heard someone shouting his name. Opening one eye, and glancing back, he saw Joey and Tar Boy thundering up behind him, snow blasting out from pounding hooves like white explosions.

"Pull on the reins. PULL ON THE REINS!" he heard the young wrangler yell. The reins. What exactly were the reins? Wait. He remembered. Those were the leather straps running to the horse's head. He checked his fingers. Nope. No reins there.

As Joey drew closer, he recognized the problem. Garth had let go of the reins. They were dangling dangerously close to Showboat's frantically thrashing front hooves.

Urging Tar Boy for more speed, the boy closed the distance between him and the terrified rider. The world was a blur of snow and ice mixed with the steady crashing of two horses blasting through a snowy meadow.

Closer, closer, closer the young wrangler came, aware of the extreme danger created by his presence. If Garth was to slip off Showboat's back, Tar Boy could run over him before Joey had a chance to alter course. But if he tried moving farther out from the runaway, coming in from the side, Showboat might see him and turn into the forest, making the situation even worse.

"HOLD ON!" Joey shouted. "DON'T LET GO OF ANYTHING!"

The rock formation was rapidly approaching, its granite face expressionless and stark in the frigid air. The young wrangler knew he had one chance to grab the reins. Frightened horses had been known to slam into fences and walls in an effort to escape danger. Hitting a solid barrier at 30 miles an hour was hard enough on a horse. For its rider, it could prove deadly.

The two animals were now side by side, racing straight for the rock wall at top speed. Taking his left foot out of the stirrup, Joey allowed himself to fall to the right, his gaze glued to Showboat's fluttering reins. Garth opened his eyes just in time to see his companion slip down into the cloud of snow being thrown up by the thundering hooves. He waited for his horse to lurch, indicating that he'd run over Joey's body, leaving it limp and broken in their wake. But the stumble didn't happen. Instead he saw Tar Boy pull up abruptly and drop back out of sight. At the same instant his horse began to slow as if fighting some unseen force. Suddenly it was over.

Then Joey jumped up and grabbed Garth's coat with both hands, pulling him violently from the saddle. As he hit the snow, he heard the wrangler shout at Showboat, slapping her hard on the rump. The animal responded by spinning around and thundering away in the direction they'd just come. Tar Boy joined her and together they raced across the meadow, away from the two teenagers.

"Are you OK?" Garth heard Joey ask, his words breathless. Looking up from where he'd fallen, he discovered they were at the base of the rocks with Joey standing over him, a worried expression on his flushed face. Garth was about to answer when up above, behind Joey, not more than 10 feet away, a furry face appeared with shining eyes that seemed to stop his heart in midbeat. A fang-filled mouth opened wide as a scream pressed him back against the snow. Joey froze, eyes wide with terror.

The three remained in their positions, unmoving. "Wendy," Joey whispered, unable to speak louder. "Wendy," Garth gasped, unable to do any better.

Another scream shook the rocks as Monty edged slightly to the left. Joey felt dizzy, his hands trembling at his sides.

"MONTY!" they heard Wendy shout as rapid footsteps approached, crunching through the snow. "MONTY! That's Joey. Don't eat him. He owes me money."

Joey closed his eyes and waited, still standing above Garth.

"Come on, Monty," the girl shouted, heading farther down the base of the rock formation. "Don't you remember Joey? He saved your neck. He saved us both from the cave. Come on now. Get your food. I've got all your favorites. You are hungry, aren't you? Sure you are. See? Animal crackers. You *love* animal crackers. You can have all the tigers and elephants, and I'll keep the zebras and rhinos. Come on, Monty. It's chow time."

Joey heard a rustling and growling overhead as he watched Garth's eyes follow the big cat as it stalked along the narrow ledge above them.

Soon he heard Wendy speaking softly to her friend some distance to his right. Garth looked up just in time to see Joey falling straight at him. Rolling to one side, he just missed being squashed into the snow by the young wrangler who dropped face-first into the white drifts. The two lay side by side for a long moment, allowing their bodies to drain the adrenalin from their bloodstreams. Finally, Garth spoke.

"Isn't there an easier way to feed a mountain lion?"

Joey's shoulders began to shake, then his whole body. He rolled onto his back, laughing as silently as he could, his face red and puffy from exertion.

Garth began laughing too as each tried to keep the other quiet. Finally, they could hold back no longer and loud, long guffaws filled the valley. Monty looked up from his newspaper-plate meal and studied the strange critters at the other end of the rock formation.

"Oh, don't bother with them," Wendy called from her waiting place nearby. "They're loonier than loons."

Slapping each other on the back, Joey and Garth began the long journey to the far end of the meadow, stumbling through the snow like drunken sailors heading home from the docks.

Tucker collapsed against a tree trunk and gasped. "Man, was that hairy or what! I thought for sure ol' Garth would be headin' home in a body bag."

Ashley nodded, trying to still her own heart. "That Joey is some kinda hero. Is that his job? To save people?"

Debbie laughed nervously, loosening her death grip on Barry's arm. "Well, not exactly. Sometimes he gets himself into situations where *he* needs saving. But that's life on a working ranch, I suppose."

Ellen stepped forward. "This is far too dangerous a place for young people," she declared, shaking her head from side to side.

"What, like New York City is in the safe zone?" Debbie shot back.

The woman pointed out into the meadow. "You don't have horses running out from under you because they got frightened by a mountain lion."

"I'll take a mountain lion over a rapist any day," Debbie stated, looking her mother in the eye for the first time since the woman had arrived. "Nature is something you grow to understand and respect. It's not so easy with people."

Wrangler Barry lifted his hand. "Why don't I take our guests a little closer to the rock formation where they can see Monty better. Come on, you guys. We'll leave Debbie and her mom to discuss the world's woes without us."

The horseman led the three teenagers away from the sleigh, heading them along the tree line in the direction of the towering rocks. Joey and Garth joined them and were soon out of earshot of the girl and her mother.

"What's your problem, Debbie?" Ellen asked. "Do you hate me so much that you can't say a civil word to me without someone ordering you to?"

The girl lowered her eyes. "I don't hate you, Mother."

"Look," the woman continued, "I made a terrible mistake a few years ago. I abandoned my family. I did a very, very selfish thing. How long do I have to pay for my error?"

Debbie sighed. "Grandpa says I should forgive you. He says I should let the past rest in peace and go on with my life. Well, that's what I've been trying to do. But you're not helping any by showing up out of nowhere. You're trying to bring the past back to life as if nothing happened. You expect me to love you just like I did years ago."

"Wendy does," the woman said softly.

"Wendy loves what you used to be, Mother. She has this bright and shiny image of you that she refuses to part with. But I know better. I remember what it was like near the end, when you and Dad would argue way into the night. I heard what you said to him back then, and you were wrong. You were dead wrong. He was willing to change for you. He was willing to work less hours so he could spend more time with you and Wendy and me. He said you could do stuff on your own, start your own business, go to school, whatever it took to make you happy. But before he had a chance to work things out, you were history, gone off with some loser who probably promised you the moon."

The girl fought back bitter tears. "Have you ever heard Daddy cry? Have you? It's such a sad sound. Well, he cried when you left, Mother. He cried and I cried and he held me and told me that everything would be all right, that he'd be both mom and dad to me. And he has been! Every minute of every day I know he loves me and is worried about me. Barry's the same way. He's just like Daddy, and I plan to spend the rest of my life with him because I can trust him, and I know he needs me."

Ellen closed her eyes as warm tears moistened her cheeks. "Oh Debbie," she said softly, "you're all grown up. You're not my little girl anymore."

"Living without you wasn't my choice, Mother," Debbie stated, a heavy sadness in her words. "But I had to survive. We all did."

The woman sank to her knees in the snow, face buried in her gloved hands. "Why can't it be like it was before?"

"Before what, Mother?"

Ellen was silent for a long moment. When she

spoke her words were but a whisper. "Before I became a fool," she said.

＊ ＊ ＊

Wendy and the others sat watching the mountain lion lick the last of his dinner off the newspaper. Garth chuckled. "I think he just ate the sports section."

Ashley shook her head. "Imagine, we just had lunch with a wild animal."

"You should eat at my house," Luisa interjected, stumbling to her feet. "Happens every day."

Wendy's brow furrowed as everyone laughed. She knew her friend wasn't joking. "Come on, you guys," she said, brushing snow from her knees. "We'd better clean up Monty's dinner table and head back to the ranch. Don't want our wildcat friend to get all hot and bothered with a bunch of people wandering around his meadow for too long."

"OK," Tucker said, standing. "Hey, thanks for showing him to us. He's one cool cat."

Luisa giggled. "You musta been talking to Ms. Cadena or Grandpa Hanson."

"Huh?"

The girl waved her hand. "Never mind. Inside joke."

As the group turned and started along the tree line, Wendy waded over to where her mountain lion friend had dined. Monty sat on his usual perch nearby, watching her roll up the newspaper and tuck it under her arm. "You did good," he heard the girl call in his direction. "You didn't eat anyone. I'm proud of you."

The big cat licked his lips and patted the rock with his front paws.

"Yeah, I know," Wendy said. "You want to go hunt food on your own. And you will, someday. For now, you can depend on me. OK?" The girl waved. "See ya in a few days."

As the group reached the trees, Joey suddenly stopped. "Hey," he declared, "where's Luisa?"

Everyone looked around. "Luisa?" Ashley called.

Wendy glanced back at the distant rocks. "There she is," she announced, pointing at the girl standing at the base of the rock formation.

Joey was about to run back to get her when Wendy stopped him. "Wait! Don't go."

The young wrangler pointed. "Whatta ya mean? Monty ain't exactly your garden variety pussy cat."

"I know," Wendy said. "But she's OK. Trust me. Monty will understand."

"Understand what?" Joey asked.

Luisa stood staring up into the rocks, the sun warm on her back. Small stones rolled from a high ledge and clattered down the face of the outcropping, landing at her feet.

"Monty?" she called. "Are you up there?"

A dark form appeared overhead and stood staring down at her. Then it began moving along the ledge. The girl could hear the soft moans and growls of the creature as it reacted to the pain in its hindquarters.

"Hurts, doesn't it?" Luisa called. "Especially after you've been still for a while."

The mountain lion maneuvered among the outcroppings, approaching ever closer to the girl waiting in the snow.

"Why does it have to hurt so much?" she continued. "Even after the scars heal, you can still feel it deep inside where no one can see." Monty walked out onto a perch just above the girl's head, his breath sending miniature clouds of vapor into the cold air. "You don't want people to know. You don't want them to know how much pain you're in. But you can't run away from it. You can't hide. The hurt follows you no matter where you go."

The animal hopped down onto a low, snow-covered rock beside Luisa, grimacing at the ache produced by the movement. Who was this creature? She wasn't the one from the cave, yet her voice carried the same softness, the same depth of feeling.

"We're soul mates, you and me," Luisa stated, slowly lifting her hand. "Did you know that, Monty? We both have been hurt bad. We both have scars." The big cat sniffed the air and stretched his neck forward until his nose was inches from the girl's outstretched glove. "Let's make a sacred promise to each other. When I hurt, I'll think of you. When you hurt, you can think of me. Then we'll be strong. Is it a deal? Will you do that?"

The mountain lion's nose touched the girl's fingers lightly. Luisa felt the creature's hot breath filtering through the soft knit cloth covering her fingers. "Yes," she whispered, "you understand. You promise, and so do I."

Then, edging closer to the animal, Luisa looked into his dark eyes. "Teach me how to scream," she said, her words choking in her throat. "Please, teach me how to scream like you. I don't know how. I only know how to hurt."

Monty studied the strange creature standing before him. Its eyes were wet and sad, its face shadowed with anguish. He felt no fear of the visitor, no anger or resentment. As with Wendy, he knew the girl meant him no harm. If only he could speak her language. If only he could communicate to her the pain and frustration he felt on cold nights when he couldn't leave the rocks to hunt. How could he tell her how much he hurt?

Suddenly, he knew what to do. Something inside stirred, telling him that he could make the world understand. He could communicate his pain. All he had to do was cry.

Drawing in a deep breath, the big cat lifted his whiskered chin and shouted his frustration toward the sky the only way he knew how.

Luisa felt the anguish behind the scream as it blasted into her face. It seemed like the sound shot straight to her heart, seizing it with powerful fingers and lifting it to her throat. In the mountain lion's earth-trembling call was all the fear and uncertainty, all the anger and hurt she'd ever experienced. If only she could cry like that. If only she could shout with such agony when her father lifted his hand again and again to strike her, driving her to the floor.

As the call echoed into the distance, Luisa leaned forward until her nose touched the creature's. "Thank you," she whispered. "Thank you for screaming for me."

With that she turned and headed out across the meadow, while Monty hobbled back to his perch where he stood and watched her figure grow smaller until the trees swallowed her up and he was alone.

❋ ❋ ❋

"Dad?"

Grandpa Hanson looked up from his partially disassembled riding mower to see his son standing in the entrance to his workshop.

"Hey, Tyler," the old man called, tossing an oily carburetor onto the table. "Come on in and close the door. Gotta keep mother nature at bay this time of year."

The lawyer stepped into the warm, cozy room and latched the wooden portal behind him. "I see you've got the Craftsman apart again."

"Yup," Grandpa Hanson nodded. "She still

runs. But it takes a lot of loving care to keep old engines sparkin' along."

The younger man laughed. "That machine pre-dates Noah. Maybe you should consider investing in something that was made in this century."

Grandpa Hanson chuckled as he wiped his hands on a greasy rag. "The longer I live, the more I feel for old things. Guess, in a way, I'm trying to preserve myself. Do you think?"

His son nodded. "So, you're saying that when you stop sparkin', I shouldn't trade you in on a newer model?"

"You got it. But for the time bein', just change my oil and scrape the rust off my cylinders. I'll be good for another hundred years."

Mr. Hanson smiled as he settled himself on the seat of the riding mower and traced the form of the steering wheel with his fingers. "Dad? I gotta ask you something."

"Shoot."

The lawyer sighed. "It's about Ellen."

"Now, Tyler, you know your mother and I aren't going to interfere with this situation. It's none of our business."

"Yeah, I know. But I need for you to make it your business for the next few minutes." He looked at his father. "I don't know what to do."

"What do you mean?"

"Well, you've been preachin' to me all my life that I'm supposed to forgive people, no matter what. I'm supposed to let go of the past, not hold grudges, let bygones be bygones. Remember?"

The old man nodded. "That's what God tells us to do."

"So," Mr. Hanson continued, "here's Ellen, who did a terrible thing by leaving me and the kids. She shacks up with this guy from Connecticut and, according to the Bible, I have every reason to divorce her, which I did."

"And?"

"And now she shows up telling me how sorry she is and asking for forgiveness. Wendy's beside herself with joy, and I . . ."

"You what?"

"I keep remembering how much she hurt us— how much she hurt me." The lawyer looked into his father's face. "What am I supposed to do, Dad? Am I supposed to forgive her and try to put this family back together again? Is that what God expects? Just how far is this forgiveness thing supposed to go?"

The old man returned his son's gaze. "And then there's Ruth Cadena, right?"

Mr. Hanson nodded slowly. "Yes. And then there's Ruth."

Grandpa Hanson leaned back in his squeaky, metal chair. "Tyler, let me give you some pieces of wisdom God has placed in my tired old brain over the years. First, forgiveness doesn't mean acceptance. You don't have to agree with what the person did to forgive them. You just have to believe that they're worth more than their sin. When God forgives us, He's not excusing our errors. He's just removing their *eternal* consequences. We, and others, still have to live with the earthly results of our errors.

"Second, for forgiveness to do its most powerful work, it has to be accepted. You can forgive Ellen until you're blue in the face, but if she doesn't accept it, you're the only one who benefits."

"Wait a minute," Mr. Hanson said, raising his hand. "How do I know if Ellen's accepted my forgiveness?"

"By the changes in her life. If we truly accept God's forgiveness, He'll see us change. We'll become what the apostle Paul calls 'a new creature.' Our hearts of stone will become hearts of flesh. Our minds will begin thinking in new, positive directions. Our actions will be different than before." Grandpa Hanson nodded in agreement with himself. "Forgiveness is potent stuff. It can make us better people."

The younger man sat thinking about his father's words. "Dad," he finally said, "do I have to remarry Ellen to show her that I've forgiven her?"

"Tyler," the old man responded with a gentle smile, "when you married her, you and she and God made a sacred promise to each other, a promise to love and honor until death. But she didn't keep her part of the bargain. She broke her word to you and to God when she gave herself to another man. The sacred promise was shattered. You see, marital unfaithfulness is more than a moral mistake. It's a person breaking their word to God Himself. Under this, and *only* this circumstance, does our heavenly Father sadly allow marriages to dissolve into divorce. But it doesn't have to be that way. He just gives us that option."

Grandpa Hanson studied his son's face. "So, it's really up to you, Tyler. You must do what you feel is best. Just know that your mother and I will be praying for you with every breath we take."

Mr. Hanson suppressed a frustrated sigh. "Why did she have to come out here? Why did she have to complicate my life?"

"*Sin* complicates life," the older man said. "It makes us all victims in the process." He walked over and placed a strong hand on his son's shoulder. "Ask God to guide you. And don't forget the power He's placed in your heart to help you face situations like this."

"What power?"

Grandpa Hanson smiled. "Love," he said. "Sometimes, when reason and knowledge fail, love can light the way."

Mr. Hanson swung his leg over the mower and stumbled to his feet. "I want to do what God wants me to do," he stated. "And I want to do what's best for me and the girls."

"Those are two in the same," his father declared. "God wants what's best for you, and He'll move heaven and earth to make sure it happens, if you ask Him for help."

"I'm asking," the young lawyer said. "I'm really asking." Then, with a weak smile and a wave, he exited the workshop, closing the door softly behind him.

CHAPTER 5

Kingdom to Come

Snow fell during the night, erasing every footprint across the broad lawns and pastures surrounding the old way station. Even now, as dawn was just beginning to lighten the eastern sky, a few flakes remained, drifting aimlessly among barren tree limbs and brushing against the sturdy horse barn and the small bridge arching across Shadow Creek.

Wendy shuffled, fully dressed, along the south wing's downstairs hallway to her mother's guest room. Pausing to straighten her ruffled blond hair with excited fingers, she smiled at her reflection in the thick-framed mirror hanging just outside the kitchen door. It was a joy to awaken at her usual before-everyone-else hour and know she'd be spending some time with her mom. Today she was especially eager to be out and about with her. In Wendy's opinion, Shadow Creek Ranch was never as beautiful as when new snow had fallen, and the ground was smooth and soft like white velvet. The view from the lookout would be even more inspiring as the sun rose, illuminating the flawless landscape with golden light. Never mind that the temperature outside was −6°. Beauty was worth numb fingers and runny noses.

She knocked softly and waited. Then she knocked again. "Mom," she whispered. "Hey, Mom."

"Wh . . . what? Who's there?"

Wendy grinned. "I'm from the IRS. Gotta talk to you about your taxes."

She heard a sleepy chuckle. "Come in, Wendy."

The girl hurried into the room then stopped short when she saw her mom peeking out from a thick pile of blankets. "Aren't you up yet?" Wendy gasped.

"Sweetheart, *God* isn't up yet," came the groggy reply.

The girl smiled. "Yes He is. He never sleeps. Grandpa said so."

Ellen yawned and smacked her lips, then reacted like something didn't taste good. "I'd forgotten how early you wake up."

"Come on, Mom," Wendy urged, "or you'll miss it."

"Miss what?"

"The sunrise. Snowed last night. It'll be beautiful from the lookout."

Ellen shifted under the covers. "Can't we watch the sunrise after breakfast?"

Wendy laughed. "Of course not. Besides, I gotta talk to you about something really important." The girl became suddenly serious. "You see, Luisa— she's one of our guests—talked some more last night, and I think I understood what she was saying. She needs someone to help her, and since you're smart and a mom and all, I thought we could figure out a plan together while we sit at the lookout. You promised you'd go with me everyday. Remember? So, hurry! Time's a wastin'! . . . Mom?"

The soft, rhythmic breathing of a sleeping person filled the room.

"Mom, I need you!"

Ellen's eyes fluttered open as she cleared her throat. "Come back a little later, sweetheart. I've gotta get my sleep. Whatever problem you have will wait. Be a good girl and close the door when you leave."

Wendy stood her ground. "You promised. You said you'd go to the lookout with me. Last night before I went to bed you—"

"Wendy, darling," Ellen interrupted, rising on one elbow, "I'll spend time with you later. OK? Now go back to bed."

The girl stared as her mother turned over and adjusted the covers. Then the woman's breathing eased back into slumber.

Quietly Wendy repeated, "You promised, Mom." Then she turned and slowly left the room.

✳ ✳ ✳

Bozeman's Main Street flowed with its usual last-day-of-the-week traffic. Grandpa Hanson carefully guided the old ranch truck along the neatly plowed thoroughfare while a country-western tune played softly on the radio. It was about a man who had wandered far and wide looking for his lost love only to find her at the gas station in his home town. But Wendy wasn't listening to the music. She had more important things to think about than lost loves and gas stations. She was on a mission, a secret mission, which, to Wendy Hanson, was the only kind worth being on.

"Where'd you say you wanted to go?" Grandpa asked, glancing at his young granddaughter.

"It's a new office building a block south of the Baxter Hotel."

"And who are you going to see?"

"Can't tell you."

"Oh, yeah. A secret. Right?"

"Right."

Grandpa Hanson surveyed the road ahead. "Well, there's the hotel. You'll have to tell me when to stop."

Wendy nodded and leaned forward in her seat. "There!" she called, pointing enthusiastically. "On the right. That brick building. You can let me out at the curb."

The old man braked his truck to a halt and

read the sign hanging above the glass and metal front doors of the modern three-story structure. Bozeman Professional Center, it proclaimed in embossed yellow letters.

"Wow. You must have important business in mind," he stated as his granddaughter unhooked her seat belt.

"Yup."

"Pick you up in an hour?"

"Yup."

"Don't be late." Grandpa Hanson revved the engine as it sputtered and almost died. "The kids at the mall will be hungry. Nothin' worse than a bunch of starvin' teenagers."

"Yup."

"I'll be down the street at the Co-op if you need me."

"OK."

"You're not going to tell me what this is all about, are you?"

"Nope."

"All right, Wendy. Have it your way. Stay inside the building 'til you see me pull up."

"I'll be there," the girl promised with a smile as she climbed down from the truck cab and pushed the passenger-side door shut with a metallic thud.

Grandpa Hanson watched her wade over the barrier of plowed snow piled along the base of the parking meters. Once inside the building, she turned and waved. The old man nodded and jammed his truck into first. With a rattle and shake, he drove away.

Wendy fished in her coat pocket for a small piece of paper and withdrew it, studying the name she'd scrawled in bright red letters earlier that day. Then she walked to the directory hanging on the wall and examined the little white letters placed in neat, professional-looking rows. There it was: Allen W. Neslund, third floor, room 310.

She entered the elevator and stood for a moment while several other people dressed in business suits and freshly pressed shirts joined her. The strong scent of aftershave and perfume almost overwhelmed her as she pressed the "3" button and waited while the little conveyance rose in response.

"May I help you?" the pretty, tastefully dressed woman sitting behind the receptionist's desk asked as Wendy approached.

"Yes, I'm Wendy Hanson, and I'm here to see Dr. Neslund," the girl declared, unzipping her coat. "I don't have a lot of time, so would you tell him I'm waiting?"

The receptionist stifled a grin. "Of course, Miss Hanson. Is he expecting you?"

"I called this morning and set up an appointment." The girl leaned forward and lowered her voice. "He is a *brain* doctor, isn't he?"

"Dr. Neslund is a practicing psychiatrist, if that's what you mean."

Wendy leaned even closer. "He knows how

to help people who are a little weird in the head, right?"

"Absolutely."

"Good," the girl said, straightening. "Then I'll see him."

"Yes ma'am," the woman nodded. "Must be an important case if he was willing to schedule you on such short notice."

"Oh, it is," Wendy stated. "It's very important."

A few moments later the woman led her into a large office with broad windows overlooking the busy street below. The sound of distant traffic was muffled, and the chairs placed at random angles about the room blossomed with thick, richly appointed fabrics and padding.

A short, plump man with thinning hair, seated behind a perfectly restored antique desk, rose when he saw the receptionist and visitor striding up to greet him.

"You must be Wendy," he said, removing his reading glasses and extending his hand warmly. "It's a pleasure to meet you. I'm Dr. Neslund."

Wendy nodded and gripped the outstretched hand firmly, causing the man to flinch slightly. "Nice office," the girl said.

"Thanks. Decorated it myself."

As the receptionist left the room, Wendy lowered herself into a nearby chair and almost disappeared within its soft folds. Pulling herself back out again, she chose a smaller, firmer bench and sat down, brushing wrinkles from her jeans.

"I like that one best too," the man admitted, walking around the desk and selecting a seat on the other side of a smooth wooden coffee table. "When you're as stout as I am," he said, pulling on his tailored suit coat and adjusting his brightly colored necktie, "overstuffed chairs can prove to be a real challenge."

Wendy smiled. "I'm used to sitting on a horse. Not much padding."

"That's right. I understand you're part of the Shadow Creek Ranch group. I like what you folks are doing for young people. Ruth Cadena is a dear friend of mine, and she keeps me up-to-date on all your visitors."

"Did she tell you about a girl named Luisa?"

The man nodded. "Yes, she did."

Wendy paused. "How much are you charging me?"

Dr. Neslund blinked. "Well . . . huh . . . my normal fees are somewhat steep, but I'm willing to work out a fair price. After all, this is an unusual case. How much do you have?"

Wendy dug into her pocket and withdrew some bills. "I've got some more in the bank, but if I withdraw it, Dad says the world as we know it will end." The girl sighed. "My father kinda exaggerates."

The psychiatrist nodded sympathetically.

"I have $16 in cash, but I'm saving some for ice cream later," Wendy stated. "How 'bout $10. Will you take $10?"

The doctor thought for a moment. "Make it $5 and you've got a deal. I'm running a special on this time slot today, and five bucks will cover things nicely."

"OK," his visitor said, passing a crinkled bill to the man's outstretched hand. "I'll need a receipt."

"Of course," Dr. Neslund responded. "I'll have my receptionist draw one up when you leave. Now, let's get down to business. I don't want to waste your money. How may I help you?"

Wendy jammed the remaining currency back into her pocket and sighed. "Why do people talk, or moan, in their sleep?"

"It's not unusual," the man stated. "As a person passes through different levels of rest, the mind can remain active, creating random images, sounds, and sometimes smells. Even animals respond to dreamed-up stimuli. Ever seen a dog chase a rabbit, even though he's curled up by the fire?"

"But Luisa talks and moans at exactly the same time each night. Midnight. And . . . there's something else."

"What?"

Wendy hesitated as if repulsed by an image in her mind. "Her back. It's all covered with lines and scars."

Dr. Neslund took in a deep breath and let it out slowly. "Wendy, I'm going to tell you something that you won't want to hear. But I think you need to know all the facts in the Luisa Adams' case.

Before you can help someone, you've got to understand the problem."

Wendy nodded. "That makes sense."

"Good," the man exclaimed. "You see, Luisa's home life isn't what it should be."

"Yeah, I know."

"Her mom is an alcoholic and drinks heavily, especially at night. Mr. Adams, Luisa's dad, works two shifts at an electronics factory and can't spend a lot of time with his daughter."

Wendy chuckled. "Good thing. Look what he does to her."

The man paused, then continued. "This leaves Luisa and her mother home alone most of the time, and a horrible pattern has developed. Her mom starts drinking at the local bars in the early evening and continues until late."

Wendy spread her hands. "So?"

Dr. Neslund looked his young client in the eye. "Most bars close at midnight."

The girl sat in silence for a long moment. Then a new image began forming in her thoughts. It was the vision of a young teenager sitting in her bed listening to the clock in the hall strike the midnight hour. Soon she hears the front door opening and her mother staggers in shouting, cursing, calling her name.

"No," Wendy said, addressing her thoughts. "That's not the way it is."

Dr. Neslund sighed. "I'm afraid so. It happens

at midnight, when her mother comes home."

Wendy's face paled. "Her mother?" she gasped. "Her mother does that to her?"

"Yes. But the girl doesn't want anyone to know, so she blocks out the facts and blames her dad. Mr. Adams is a hardworking, honest man who wants to take Luisa away from his wife, but the law won't allow it. If he was to separate them, Mrs. Adams could have him thrown in jail. So he's forced to stand back and watch it happen—and get blamed for the abuse. Luisa firmly believes her father is the cause of her pain when, in fact, his life is being destroyed by it too."

Wendy stared motionless, stunned by what she'd heard. When she spoke, her words were strained. "What can I do to help her, Dr. Neslund? When she cries out at midnight, my heart aches way deep down inside. Last night I heard her say, 'It hurts, it hurts.' Then she moaned, 'I can't live. I can't live anymore.' It scared me. It scared me so much that I wanted someone to help, so Ms. Cadena told me to talk to you, and now you tell me this." The girl began to sob quietly. "What am I supposed to do now? I'm so frightened for Luisa. Her back is horrible, and she hurts so much. Please help her! Please, she's so sad inside!"

Dr. Neslund hurried over and wrapped gentle arms around her shoulders. "Go ahead and cry, Wendy," he said softly. "It's the first step any human being needs to take in order to touch the

117

life of another person who's experiencing such anguish. Let your heart break for Luisa. Then we can begin to heal you both."

The man rocked back and forth, holding the girl tightly as her choking sobs filled the room. Outside the traffic moved along Main Street in ordered rows, their drivers busy with Friday chores and appointments.

Dr. Neslund knew Luisa Adams finally had a real chance to break away from her smothering burden of abuse, for in this world there is no more powerful therapy for a tortured mind than to come in contact with a friend who cares enough to cry.

❊ ❊ ❊

Mr. Hanson paused on his way to the den. "Hear that?" he asked, lifting his hand.

Lizzy Pierce stopped beside him and tilted her head to one side. "I don't hear anything."

"Exactly!" the lawyer stated. "That's the sound of peace and quiet, a condition this Station doesn't experience often during daylight hours."

Lizzy grinned. "You kinda like it when most everybody's in Bozeman, huh?"

"Listen," the man gasped, a blissful expression spreading across his face. "I can hear the clock ticking. I didn't even know it ticked. And the refrigerator in the kitchen—it hums. Amazing!"

The old woman shook her head. "Tyler Hanson, you're going crazy right before my eyes."

Mr. Hanson brightened. "Wow. I understood what you said. I don't have to respond with, 'What? Say again? Excuse me?' Your words were clear and easy to comprehend. No one else was talking. No kid was screaming from the balcony. It's a miracle. I CAN HEAR!"

Lizzy waved her hand in the air. "I'm getting away from you before I catch whatever you've got. I for one enjoy the noisy chatter of young people in the Station. Kinda livens things up a bit."

Mr. Hanson laughed. "Oh, don't call for the guys in white lab coats. I'm not takin' a dip in Loony Bay. It's just nice to listen to one sound at a time." He lifted a finger. "Like that one," he whispered. "What was it?"

Lizzy blinked. "Someone just flushed a toilet."

At that moment Wrangler Barry walked out of the hall bathroom. Mr. Hanson hurried over to him. "Thank you, thank you," the lawyer breathed, grabbing the horseman's hand and shaking it briskly. "That was beautiful, just beautiful!"

Barry's eyes opened wide. "Huh . . . sure. You're welcome. Glad you liked it."

The lawyer gave the wrangler's hand another emotional squeeze and hurried off, mumbling something about the mystery of the human ear. Barry glanced at Lizzy, who stood shaking her head and sighing. Then, with a shrug, he walked into the den.

✳ ✳ ✳

When the Sabbath arrived once again at Shadow Creek Ranch, the four young guests noticed a familiar change taking place. The hurried pace of ranch life slowed. Conversations turned from sports, schools, and shopping to discussions about the things of nature, and of God. Grandpa Hanson announced that the entire day was to be spent concentrating on one central theme—worship and praise to the Power who made all things beautiful. That was even the topic of the sermon presented at the little country church just off the main highway leading into Bozeman.

Tucker, Garth, Ashley, and Luisa sat next to the others, spellbound by the heartfelt words spoken by the preacher known affectionately as Pastor Webley. He was a young man, father of a small son, and was married to a wife who vigorously played the little electric organ for the service. To watch her, you'd think she was seated at a lofty console surrounded by towering stacks of shiny pipes and rows upon rows of white and black keys. Even though the music created by the instrument's little speakers was sufficient to support the singing, it hardly matched the enthusiasm and feeling expressed by the skillful fingers sweeping up and down the single, somewhat battered keyboard.

Near the end of his sermon, Pastor Webley said something that particularly caught Luisa's attention. Holding up an old, worn Bible, the young minister read these words: "And God shall wipe away all tears from their eyes; and there shall be no more death, neither sorrow, nor crying, neither shall there be any more pain: for the former things are passed away." The man reverently closed the book and stared out at his little congregation. "That passage," he said, "found in Revelation 21:4, is the ultimate testimony of God's power and love. Sin, sickness, violence, and heartache will have no place in His kingdom to come."

Pastor Webley leaned forward and rested his elbows on the tall wooden podium. "Can you imagine a world with no pain?" he asked. "God can. Can you imagine a day, a week, a whole year without one tear in it? God can. And He's asking you not only to *imagine* such a world, but to expect it, plan for it, get ready to live in it! That's the type of world He's preparing for you right now, right this moment—a universe filled with perfect joy and perfect freedom from all sin and sorrow."

The man straightened. "How many of you, today, would like to tell your God that you're looking forward to His new world? How many of you are tired of living in Satan's backyard and long for something better, something that will place a smile on your lips and a chuckle in your heart? That's what the hope presented in this book can do, even when things look dark and depressing. If you'd like to tell God that you want to be a citizen of the kingdom, stand to your feet—no, *jump* to your feet right now and tell Him you want to be among those who will someday make that journey with Him from darkness into light."

The congregation rose as one body amid the sounds of shuffling feet and squeaking floor-boards. Luisa noticed that Wendy was one of the first to leap out of her pew and stand smiling up at the minister. The visitor didn't know what to do. All this religion stuff was new to her, but the preacher's words had sounded so hopeful, so full of joy. A world free from pain and tears? She'd been imagining such a place for years, but she thought she was the only one with such dreams.

Wendy glanced down at the girl who still remained seated. "Come on, Luisa," she urged in a whisper. "We can be neighbors in God's kingdom. Hope you don't mind living next to a zoo!"

Luisa hesitated.

"Don't you want to tell God that you're looking forward to heaven?" her friend questioned softly.

Heaven? Was that the name of the world for which she'd been longing? Perhaps it did exist. Who could know for sure? At least it sounded nice.

The girl nodded and rose to her feet. Hey, why not. She'd play the game with everyone else. If heaven ended up no more than a fleeting dream, it was a nice dream. And anything was better than the life she was presently living.

Luisa listened as the minister's wife played the opening chords of the closing hymn. As the people started singing, a strange sensation crept through her being. She felt a new expectancy, a new excitement, an emotion she'd never experienced before. It felt good to stand up for something hopeful. Even if all this talk of God and of a world to come where there'd be no pain and tears turned out to have no foundation, for one shining moment she felt happy. As the congregation sang, Luisa allowed herself to almost believe that such a place truly existed, and that for some strange, unexplainable reason, she was being invited to live there.

She glanced over at Wendy, who stood watching Joey sing, his determined tones about two notes off key. This strange person with the short, golden hair seemed to believe, as did all the other year-round residents at Shadow Creek Ranch. Maybe there was something to this heaven idea after all. Maybe.

✳ ✳ ✳

"Mrs. Hanson, I believe that you have set a new standard of excellence when it comes to Sabbath dinners. My stomach will be in ecstasy for the next five days over your astonishing lentil casserole with mushroom sauce." Pastor Webley pushed his chair back from the table and grinned broadly. "My wife and I certainly look forward to our visits with you kind folk here on Shadow Creek Ranch."

"Well, thank you, pastor," Grandma Hanson responded with a shy nod. "After that lovely sermon you delivered this morning, we just had to show our appreciation."

Wendy took a sip of milk and wiped her upper lip with her sleeve. "I, for one, don't plan to sit around on a cloud playing a silly harp when I get to heaven. No sir. Me and Samantha are gonna start our own collection of intergalactic animals. Then we'll charge admission and make a fortune!"

"I'll be your first customer," Pastor Webley promised. "How 'bout you, Miss Debbie, got any plans for heaven?"

The girl thought for a moment. "Choir robes," she said with a twinkle in her eye. "I'm going to design and produce choir robes for all the heavenly singers."

Joey put down his spoon and gazed out the nearby window. "I'm going to be a soloist and hit all those fancy notes without missing a one."

Wendy about choked on her spoonful of pudding. "You? Sing?" She turned to Samantha. "Maybe we should locate our zoo a little farther out of town."

"*Way* out of town," Samantha stated firmly.

Pastor Webley smiled. "How 'bout you, Tucker? What're your plans for heaven?"

The boy blinked. "I . . . I don't know. Fly around, I guess. Haven't given it much thought."

"Few people do," the pastor sighed. "But that's the beauty of heaven. We can start planning for our life there right now, here on earth. How 'bout you, Garth? Any ideas?"

"Yeah, sure, like God's gonna let me in."

"Why wouldn't He?"

The boy glanced about the table. "I ain't exactly no monk, if you catch my drift. Heaven's for good people, right?"

"Sorta," the man responded. "Heaven is for sinful people who've allowed Christ's goodness to cover their sins. We'll always make mistakes, but if we live our lives getting to know Jesus better and better, doing our best to keep God's commandments, and trusting in His forgiveness, we're in. It's as simple as that."

The boy frowned, then his expression relaxed into a smile. "Well, whatever," he said. "Let's say I do make it to heaven. Then I'm gonna open a store and sell T-shirts and baseball cards. And no one'll rob the place 'cause guns ain't allowed in heaven, right?"

"Right," the minister affirmed.

"And I'm gonna own my own basketball team, and we'll play all over the universe and beat the pants off every team 'cause we're just that good."

"Save me a front row seat at the playoffs!" Pastor Webley chimed in.

"You got it," Garth promised with a firm handshake across the table.

"I'm not into sports," Ashley announced, clearing her throat shyly. "But I do like music. Maybe I'll sing in Joey's choir or somethin'." She brightened. "I know. I'll be the pianist. My mom got me a piano four years ago. I mean, it's not new or anything, and some of the keys stick, but I can play a couple tunes."

"Perfect!" the young minister exclaimed. "My wife can give you lessons." He closed his eyes and lifted his hands out in front of him. "I can see it now, a huge choir with Joey as the soloist. You're seated at the big, 14-foot Steinway, fingers poised above the keys, waiting for the downbeat." He clapped his hands together. "Oh, how beautiful the music will be! How inspiring!"

Wendy's eyebrows rose. "And Joey'll sing a solo?" Turning to Samantha, she whispered, "I wonder if Pluto's available."

The younger girl nodded thoughtfully.

"And you, Luisa?" the minister invited softly. "What will heaven be for you?"

Wendy glanced down at her plate, not wanting to show her intense interest in what the girl would say. She heard her friend sigh. "I liked what you read this morning during the service—you know, about how there'll be no more pain in heaven? I have . . . a friend who has a rough time at home. She gets kinda beat up a lot. Heaven sounds like a great place . . . for my friend."

Wendy glanced over at Ms. Cadena, who tilted her head slightly in response.

"But what about *you*, Luisa?" the young minister pressed. "Isn't there anything you're looking forward to?"

The girl hesitated, then nodded. "I want to

sleep all night without dreaming," she said softly. Looking over at the young minister, she added, "Do you think that's possible?"

Pastor Webley smiled. "In the Bible God says, 'Come unto me, all ye that labour and are heavy laden, and I will give you rest.' That passage is found in Matthew 11:28. If a good night's sleep is what you want most, then, to you, heaven will be a peaceful place to slumber where soft breezes will blow across your face, and nature will be hushed while you rest in the safe, secure arms of Jesus."

Luisa was silent for a long moment. "Yes," she said, "that's what I want heaven to be."

Wendy's eyes opened wide as her bottom jaw dropped. That was it! That was the answer! She looked back at Ms. Cadena, who sat staring at her expectantly. The girl moved her left hand forward across her napkin and slowly, unseen by everyone else at the table, made a fist and lifted her thumb straight up. It was a signal Ruth understood. Her young friend had a plan, and she knew that once Wendy Hanson got a notion in her head, absolutely nothing could stop it.

The woman winked and turned back to Pastor Webley, who was continuing his discussion with those seated around him at the big dinner table. Wendy glanced over at Luisa. The girl sat silent and thoughtful, staring down at her half-eaten chocolate pudding. For the first time, Wendy knew she could do something to help her hurting friend.

It would take a combination of the ideas presented by Dr. Neslund and the pastor. Wendy closed her eyes as thoughts swirled through her mind. If she was careful, if she took her time and planned each step, she could break through Luisa's deep sadness. Her fist tightened in determination. Maybe, just maybe, she could even stop the girl's anguished midnight cries.

CHAPTER 6

The Race

"Tyler, we've got to talk." Ellen stood in the doorway where she'd been watching her ex-husband busily keying in data into his computer.

The man turned and smiled over at her. "Good morning, Ellen," he said quietly. "Come in and have a seat. I'm getting ready to E-mail some research material to the New York office. Won't take but a second to make the connection."

Ellen saw him move and click the mouse as screen images flickered. Then the unmistakable sound of a modem dialing out, followed by several scratchy signals echoing from the phone lines, announced that an electronic link had formed between Mr. Hanson's powerful desktop computer and another machine just like it in a downtown Manhattan office.

Spinning around in his tall, leather chair, the man folded his hands over his lap and sat back comfortably with a sigh. "Ah, modern technology," he said. "This'll take a few minutes, so I'm all yours. What do you want to talk about?"

Ellen lowered her eyes, then returned the lawyer's gaze. "Us," she said.

"OK. What about us?"

The woman frowned slightly. "Why have you been so nice to me the last couple days?"

Mr. Hanson chuckled. "Is that a problem? Should I be mean or vindictive instead?"

"No. I mean, yes. I mean—" She crossed her arms over her chest. "What're you trying to do?"

"Nothing," the lawyer responded. "Just helping you make a decision."

"Me?"

Mr. Hanson shifted his position. "Look, Ellen. I know you didn't get on an airplane, which you hate to do, and fly all the way out here to Montana just to enjoy a snowy holiday in the mountains. You haven't been a part of this family for years. And then you show up suddenly expecting to pick up where we and the kids left off. There had to be a reason, and you made it quite clear, especially to Ruth Cadena."

"Oh, and I suppose you're thinking I came out here to win you back," Ellen asserted. "Aren't you being a touch over-confident?"

The lawyer shook his head. "At first that's exactly what I thought. Then I did some soul-searching, and a lot of praying. Even determined not to put up a fight if those were your intentions. Wendy's nuts about you, Ellen. She always has been. And there's nothing in this world more important to me than the happiness of my two little girls."

Ellen lowered her gaze.

"And remember," the man continued, "you left me. *You* stopped loving *me,* not the other way around. I still have feelings for you. Yeah, that's right. Buried deep under a suffocating load of hurt and anger is a lot of tenderness for the woman I fell in love with almost 20 years ago. I planned my life around you, and once those plans were under way, they were hard to stop." Mr. Hanson lifted his hands and motioned about the room. "This . . . this whole idea of living in Montana came about because the plans I'd made in New York required you in my life. Here, they don't. Here, in this office, in this way station, I'm free to dream about a future without you in it. I'm even free to consider loving someone else the way I once loved you, if that's what I choose."

Mr. Hanson stood and walked across the room. Seating himself on the office couch next to his ex-wife, he added, "So here's the deal I was going to offer you, Ellen. This time you'd have to make your plans around me. This time you'd have to accept more than the dreams of a young lawyer just starting out. I already know my place in life and what I want to do. It's right here in Montana working in this office and helping my dad run a ranch for troubled kids like those building a snowman in the front yard."

The lawyer hesitated. "I was even willing to forgive you for the past," he said softly. "But you're not ready for the responsibility that comes with forgiveness. You're not ready to change, Ellen, to become someone you're not."

"What do you mean by that?" she shot back, anger in her eyes.

"I've been watching you," Mr. Hanson stated calmly. "I've been seeing how you relate to Wendy, Debbie, me, the whole ranch family. You haven't changed. You're still playing at being a mother, and you want to play at being my wife. And, most telling of all, I've come to realize the true reason behind your surprise visit."

"And what might that be?"

The lawyer looked deep into his companion's eyes. "You're not here to win back my love," he said. "You're here simply to see if you can."

Ellen sat in silence, thoughtfully studying his expressionless face. Outside, the muffled sounds of happy shouts and laughter drifted in the cold mountain air.

Sudden tears glistened in her eyes as she slowly stood to her feet. Walking to the door she paused. "You must hate me," she said without turning.

Mr. Hanson shook his head. "Sometimes I wish I did. It would make seeing you a lot easier."

Ellen lifted her chin as if to speak, then lowered it again. Without looking back she left the room just as the computer announced that the transmission had ended. The lawyer moved to the keyboard and closed the program, then sat for a long time staring at the blank screen.

❄ ❄ ❄

Luisa watched as Wendy hurriedly gathered the newspaper and other scraps from Monty's afternoon meal. "Look at this," Wendy called back to her, lifting a half-chewed loaf of bread for her companion to see. "He didn't eat it all. That's a good sign. Must be getting around better. Maybe even got himself a mouse or found a rabbit carcass. Doctor said he'd start hunting more when the pain lessened." She looked up into the rock formation where the big mountain lion sat staring back at her. "Good cat," she called. "You're such a smart feline. Been snackin', haven't ya!"

Monty licked his lips and pawed the rock with his claws. "Oh, don't worry," the girl stated warmly, "I'll still come and make up for what you can't get on your own. You don't have to feel rejected or anything." She paused, casting a quick glance at the tree line where Luisa waited. Addressing the mountain lion, she added, "That's like God, you know. Grandpa says the good Lord finishes what we start, if we can't do it ourselves."

"The good Lord?" Luisa laughed, overhearing her. "Hey Wendy, you sound like Pastor Webley, preachin' to a mountain lion."

"Yeah, I guess I do," Wendy chuckled, walking toward the trees. "But nobody, not even a mountain lion, should ever feel like no one cares about their problems. Whenever I'm in trouble, and believe me, that's often, I know God sees me and hears my prayers. Makes me feel a little better."

"You actually talk to God?"

"Sure."

"How?"

Wendy shrugged. "I just . . . talk, and He listens. Simple."

"What do you say to Him?"

"Oh, I don't know. Anything that pops into my mind. I even told Him I was mad at Him once. He took it quite well."

Luisa thought for a moment. "You ever talked to Him when you were scared?"

Wendy laughed. "Are you kidding? Tons of times!"

"Does He answer?"

"Well, not in words. He puts thoughts in my mind or helps me decide important stuff. Sometimes He gets other people to do His talking for Him. You gotta listen carefully, though, or you'll miss it."

Monty growled from his perch up on the rocks. "Maybe that's God talking through Monty," Luisa joked.

Wendy grinned. "Nah. That's Monty talking through Monty. He's just saying 'Thank you for the delicious meal and please come again in a couple days or I'll scream at the moon 'til you show up.'"

"He said all that in one little growl?" Luisa laughed, a twinkle in her eye.

"Sure," Wendy nodded with a mischievous smile. "He also said that he likes you and hopes you'll come see him again before you go back to Orlando, where it's hot and everyone wears bikinis."

Luisa and Wendy began walking along the tree line, heading toward the far end of the meadow where their two horses waited. "You're pretty good at this translation stuff," the girl from Florida stated.

"Yeah, I am," Wendy agreed. "Just got to know how to listen."

Monty watched his human friends climb aboard their horses and, with a wave in his direction, disappear into the forest. He sniffed the air, yawned, and headed for his den to sleep off the big lunch he'd just enjoyed. Tonight he'd try hunting in the meadow once more. The food the girl brought was fine, but nothing tasted better than a meal he'd tracked and caught all by himself. After all, even wounded mountain lions have their pride.

❋ ❋ ❋

"OK, you guys, gather 'round." Grandpa Hanson stood on the bed of the ranch's pickup truck, waving his arms in invitation. "You know the rules. But just in case someone's had a brain

135

meltdown since this morning when we went over them, allow me a quick review."

The entire group of young people from Shadow Creek Ranch paused in their preparations and turned to face him. It was midafternoon. Overhead the sun shone brightly in a clear, azure sky, turning the high pasture and its deep snow into an expanse of almost blinding beauty. The old man smiled as he tried to shush Pueblo, the ranch's big watchdog, who insisted on barking excitedly at his feet.

"Rule one: the last mile of this race may be run on horseback if you so choose. I noticed that each team positioned saddled horses at a location exactly that distance from the Station as determined by our official race coordinator, my one and only son, Tyler Hanson."

"Yeah!" the assembled contestants cheered, their voices carrying in the crisp, mountain air. Mr. Hanson bowed from the waist with a flourish.

"Rule two," the speaker continued: "you may not use a motorized conveyance during any portion of the race."

"What's a con . . . con . . . ?" Samantha tilted her head to one side and looked up at her adopted brother questioningly. Joey chuckled. "That means you can't drive a car or snowmobile or anything like that while you're in the race."

"But I'm only 6 years old," the little girl retorted.

"Then you can't *ride* in anything that has a motor," Joey told her.

Samantha frowned. "Then I guess helicopters are out."

"And rule three: everything you use to reach your horses must still be in your possession when you get to that spot."

The contestants nodded and moved quickly to the starting line—a shallow ditch dug by Mr. Hanson's boot in the meadow's freshly fallen snow.

Each team had previously determined in their own minds the fastest method for getting from the high pasture to the valley far below, where their horses waited. Tucker had decided that racing down mountains wasn't something he'd been relishing since birth so had volunteered to stay with Wrangler Barry in the lower meadow to keep the animals primed and ready for the contestants when, and if, they arrived.

Joey slipped his feet into a pair of snowshoes and adjusted the straps. Garth did the same, allowing his more experienced teammate to check the bindings carefully. They straightened the coiled ropes slung over their shoulders and took in a deep breath of air. Come what may, they were going to win this thing.

Wendy ran a hand along the shiny runners of her sled and made sure her ice skates were snugly encased in her backpack. "You ready?" she asked her teammate, Luisa, who was admiring the smooth runners of her own tall, brightly painted sled.

"Ready!" came the quick reply. "And I can

hardly wait 'till we get to the creek so we can start skating. Glad I took lessons when I was younger. Mom used to say I could be a champion if I wanted. She encourages me a lot, you know."

Wendy nodded and looked away, then smiled. "She sounds like my dad," the girl stated. "He's always tellin' me how wonderful I am. Your dad ever say stuff like that?"

Luisa kicked at a snow clod. "I suppose."

The girls figured to take advantage of the thick ice covering the creek at the bottom of Castle Mountain. They both hoped no one had noticed how inviting the smooth surface had looked the day before during an outing to visit the Dawsons and planned for this event.

With a solid click, Debbie's boots fastened themselves into the bindings of her cross-country skis. Ashley knelt over her own pair, making sure her feet were snug and secure in their constraints. Across their backs the girls wore the objects of many a sidelong glance from the other contestants.

"Afraid you're gonna have a flat?" Joey called, eyeing the two firmly inflated inner tubes adorning his competitors.

Debbie smiled. "Spring's coming," she said sweetly. "You and Garth try to finish the race before the wake robins bloom."

Samantha looked about expectantly. "I'm going to win because I have a secret plan."

The others tried to ignore the little girl's confident remark, concentrating instead on the plans they'd devised to get them to the way station long before the others.

"I'm acting as Samantha's teammate," Grandpa Hanson announced, "but she'll do all the work. I'll just be following her in the truck."

"She's takin' the logging road back," Joey whispered to Garth just loud enough for Samantha to hear. "And all she's got is a saucer." He leaned forward. "She's dead meat!"

Garth nodded and grinned. "Yeah, like, a 6-year-old is a threat to two guys with ropes. But we won't laugh at her when she finally shows up at the finish line, right?"

Joey suppressed a grin and tried to look worried. "We wouldn't want to hurt her feelings, now would we?"

"YES!" they both shouted.

Samantha rolled her eyes then looked menacingly at them. Pointing a gloved finger in their direction, she whispered back, "It ain't over 'till it's over."

"OK teams, get on your marks," Grandpa Hanson called. Everyone hovered over the line in the snow. "Get set." Bodies leaned forward expectantly as the old man lifted his hand. Dropping it suddenly, he shouted, "GO!"

Loose snow flew in all directions as the contestants burst across the line. Joey and Garth headed directly for the far end of the pasture, where the land dropped suddenly to a lower valley. Their scheme was simple. They'd snowshoe across the soft, flat areas and rappel down the three or four rock outcroppings they knew waited between them and the horses. Their team would be traveling in a straight line, while everyone else was forced to zig and zag down the mountains.

Wendy and Luisa's plan was different. They'd zip along the hard-packed deer and elk trails on their sleds. Their route was the longest, but speed would be their ally.

Where the forest path curved past Shadow Creek, they'd both slip on their ice skates, sling the sleds over their shoulders, and quickly cover the distance to the horses.

Debbie and Ashley had designed another approach. They'd ski down the southern slopes, heading for the pasture. Where the hillsides got rough, they'd jump on the large inner tubes and speed over the surface, letting gravity and nerve carry them along.

Samantha stood watching her friends disappear. "Now," she announced, picking up her little silver saucer, "it's time for my secret plan." She turned and began running for the logging road, Pueblo barking at her heels. Grandpa Hanson and his lawyer son followed some distance behind her in the pickup truck. Soon the meadow was empty of all racers, leaving the wind to gently stroke the mountain snows.

❄ ❄ ❄

Ruth Cadena looked up from her notebook computer and saw that Ellen had entered the big, cozy den and was standing by the warm fireplace. "Are they here yet?" she asked, glancing out the window.

"No," Ellen responded with a shake of her head. "Mrs. Pierce and Grandma are sitting all bundled up like a couple of woolen mountains on the top steps. They'll call when the first team appears at the end of the driveway."

Ruth smiled over at the other woman. "It's been nice having you here during our winter camp. Wendy can't stop talking about how much fun it is to have her mother so close by. She loves you very much. So does Debbie, I'm sure."

Ellen laughed quietly. "Wendy loves; Debbie tolerates. I'm not exactly on the A list with my eldest."

"I'm sorry."

"Yeah. Me too."

Ruth glanced down at the screen. "And Tyler? Any headway?"

"What do you mean?"

Ms. Cadena reached up and gently closed the computer. "Do I sense reconciliation in the air?"

"That's . . . what I wanted to talk to you about," Ellen replied.

Ruth lifted her hands. "Hey. It's none of my business."

"You're wrong, Ruth," the woman replied, her

voice calm. "It's very much your business, because I know you're in love with Tyler."

The youth worker glanced out the window. "I . . . I admire your ex-husband very much."

"You love him. I know it, and he knows it."

"Ellen, you're embarrassing me," Ms. Cadena said shyly. "Please don't think that I'm trying to turn my relationship with Tyler into a contest between you and me. He's a kind and gentle man, and I've allowed myself to grow very fond of him."

The woman by the fire rolled her eyes and sighed. "Ruth, stop. You don't have to guard my feelings. Heaven knows I haven't exactly been very careful with yours. You deserve better."

Ms. Cadena pushed back into her chair. "What are you trying to say, Ellen?"

"I'm trying to say that . . . that I'm sorry for being such a pain over the last two weeks. I came out here thinking I'd sweep everyone off their feet—you know, the returning mom and long-lost lover, stuff like that. But instead, it was I who was swept away—by this ranch, by the people who live and work here, by what it stands for." She pointed out the window. "My ex-husband is out there spending the day with a bunch of kids who, three weeks ago, would've tried to lift his wallet, or worse. His office upstairs is empty. All the machines are turned off."

She paused. "And you know the most disturbing part? He promised he'd do that for me, but I was too impatient. I wanted results right now, not later. So I took matters into my own hands and tried to create a world for myself where everything revolved around me. I was willing to sacrifice whatever it took to get what I wanted, and in doing so threw away my most precious possession, my family."

Ruth raised her hand in an almost pleading gesture. "Why are you telling me all this?"

"Because—" Ellen hesitated. "Because they're your family now. You're part of their world, and I'm not. I never can be again."

Ms. Cadena stared at the woman for a long moment. "What about Wendy?" she asked.

Ellen closed her eyes. "She's growing up, just like Debbie. Soon, very soon, she'll begin to understand that her mom isn't the perfect angel she imagines her to be. I don't want to be around when that happens. It would break my heart even more."

The tall clock resting against the far wall chimed out the hour. As the sound faded, Ruth Cadena looked over at Tyler's ex-wife. "I'm sorry it worked out this way, Ellen. You deserve to be happy. Everyone does."

The woman nodded. "Sometimes," she said softly, "happiness is where you least expect it. For me, it was mixed up with piles of laundry and visits to the grocery store, or simmering on the stove late-night meals prepared for a husband who was learning that work isn't everything. Funny how you can miss something so beautiful when it's right there in your arms." She glanced at Ruth and smiled. "Tyler deserves something better than me. He deserves you."

With that, she turned and quietly left the room.

* * *

Grandma Hanson and Lizzy sat bundled together on the top step of the Station's front porch, eyes focused on the long driveway running from the building to the logging road.

"Look!" Mrs. Pierce called out as a dark form took shape a half-mile to the east. "Here comes somebody."

"I think I see two riders," Grandma Hanson shouted. "No, four. Wait, six! I see all six riders."

The two women glanced down at the finish line, where Mr. Hanson waited, blowing warm air into his cupped hands. "Look at 'em come," he shouted. "Everyone's plan worked exactly the same."

Thundering hoofbeats reverberated across the little valley as the horses swept down the driveway and crossed the finish line amid clouds of swirling snow, some riders holding on for dear life, eyes closed, mouths pressed into thin, pale lines.

Joey jumped from Tar Boy even before the big animal had come to a halt. "We won, we won!" he shouted, grabbing Garth and pulling him from his horse. The two danced a strange jig right there in the snow.

"You're crazy!" Debbie countered, trying to control her horse while helping Ashley dismount. "We were ahead by a nose."

"No, we got here first," Wendy argued, throwing Luisa a high five and missing.

"Hold on, you guys," Mr. Hanson interrupted with a big grin. "I'm supposed to decide who the winner is, remember?"

"Well?" the six out-of-breath contestants chorused.

"Well?" a young voice called from the porch.

The group spun around to see Samantha sitting snugly between Grandma Hanson and Lizzy, wrapped in a blanket with only her nose and eyes showing. Joey blinked. "I don't believe it! *Samantha* got here first? How?"

"My secret plan," the little girl smiled, unwrapping herself and standing proudly to her feet.

Debbie flopped into a snowbank. "You mind telling us what you did to get here so fast?"

"Dog power," Samantha declared.

"Dog power?" the riders gasped.

"Yup. Grandpa Hanson made a harness for Pueblo, and I tied my saucer to it. That critter ran all the way home." The ranch's watchdog appeared at the top of the steps, jowls covered with a white substance. "Pueblo loves ice cream," Samantha announced. "So, I told him he could have a big bowl if he got me here first. Boy did we really zoom down that mountain, and I mean FAST!"

"But . . . but . . ." Joey's voice faltered as he dropped to his knees. "She did it. She followed the rules and beat us fair and square."

Wendy moaned. "Dog power. And there we were ice skating our feet off while Samantha sat like a queen being pulled by a mangy mutt with a killer ice-cream habit."

Grandpa Hanson appeared at the front door chuckling. "Don't feel bad, guys," he encouraged. "Each team formulated a plan and stuck with it. Important thing is, you finished the race."

The old man rubbed his chin thoughtfully. "Kinda reminds me of a verse in the New Testament."

Wendy nudged Luisa. "That's unusual."

Her friend giggled.

"The apostle Paul said he 'fought a good fight and finished the course.' Well," Grandpa Hanson patted Samantha on the top of her knit cap, "we're all in a race to heaven. Been given rules to follow, too. But the route we choose, ah, that's up to us. It's somethin' we gotta work out for ourselves."

The young people nodded, then wearily returned to their horses. They had snowshoes, skis, sleds, rope, and inner tubes to retrieve a mile back.

As they rode along, retracing their steps to where Tucker and Wrangler Barry waited in the distant pasture, Grandpa Hanson's words kept echoing in their ears. *Life's a race. God sets the rules. Each must run the course based on a plan he or she believes will help them finish successfully.*

Joey called over to his companions. "You guys wouldn't happen to know where I could find a really, *really* big dog?"

Wendy chuckled. "You're sitting on one."

The boy sighed. "Very funny, Miss Hanson. I didn't see you crossing the finish line before Sam either."

"If I'd been ridin' Early I would've. Besides, me and Luisa let her win," Wendy countered. "She's just a kid. Didn't want to get her all depressed and stuff."

"Yeah, right."

Luisa listened to the banter tossed back and forth by the two riders as they headed down the long driveway. Suddenly their words didn't sound so frightening to her, because she knew that deep in their hearts they cared for each other.

Echoes of other words drifted in her thoughts. *I gotta get you away from here. You can't stay with her. She hurts you.* Were they spoken by someone who cared for her? Wasn't he the one that caused the pain?

Luisa shook her head, trying to clear her thoughts. Who could help her figure out all this mess? Who could she talk to? Tomorrow she'd be leaving, heading back to Orlando, away from Wendy, away from Monty, away from a place where she'd felt at peace for the first time in many, many years. And then there was heaven, a dream that just might come true, after all. How could she prepare for a race with such a wonderful finish line?

"Are you OK?" she heard Wendy ask.

"Yeah," the girl breathed.

"You were frowning."

"I was?"

Wendy adjusted her grip on her horse's reins. "My dad says if you frown too much, your face will become permanently wrinkled. My grandma's face is wrinkled, but I've never seen her frown in all my life. Sometimes dads say stupid things."

"Yeah, sometimes," Luisa breathed. "But . . ."

"But what?" Wendy chuckled.

"But . . . not always. Right?"

For a long moment Wendy stared at the girl. "Yes," she said softly, "not always."

The group continued their journey back to the meadow, horses' hooves crunching through the snow.

CHAPTER 7

Memories

It was a tired and happy group that gathered around the big fireplace in the den that night. Morning would bring suitcases, hugs, and good-byes. But now was a time for remembering.

Winter camp was drawing to a close, and no one, especially the four guests who'd left faraway cities to spend two weeks among the mountains, wanted the adventure to end.

"Can I take Showboat home with me?" Garth asked plaintively as he gazed into the flickering flames, marshmallow browning at the end of a crooked wire clothes hanger.

"Sure," Ms. Cadena chuckled, "you can take anything you want as long as it fits in the overhead compartment in the airplane."

Garth laughed. "Can't you just see me tryin' to stuff that ol' Appaloosa into that tiny space? The flight attendants might not approve."

Tucker nodded. "I was kinda hopin' to pack the

view from my upstairs window into my suitcase, except it won't fit, either. Wendy took a picture with her camera for me the other day—you know, after the new snow fell? She said she'd make an enlargement for me in her darkroom. I'm gonna get it framed and hang it in my bedroom in Chicago. All I see from my window there is a brick wall."

Ashley sighed. "I'm going to miss this place. I feel safe here, even when I'm barrelin' down the valley on a horse or hanging on to Joey's sleigh. It's a feeling I don't often get in my neighborhood back home. Yeah, I'm going to remember Shadow Creek Ranch forever. If there is a heaven like Pastor Webley said, I think it'll be just like here."

"Only not as *cold!*" Luisa interjected. "And," the girl added, "there'll be no hurt mountain lions in the rocks. Pain will be gone, you know?"

Wendy giggled. "Now *you* sound like Pastor Webley."

"Hey," Luisa said, nodding, "I guess I do."

Ms. Cadena studied their faces as they gazed into the flames and enjoyed the taste of roasted marshmallows. "What did you learn here?" she asked the group. "What stands out most in your minds?"

Tucker shifted his position on the thick rug. "The mountains," he said. "They're so . . . so big, and I'm so small. Made me realize just how awesome nature is, how beautiful, too. Now, when the city starts to get me really depressed, I'll remember Montana, and the big spaces all around."

"I liked the way Joey took care of the horses," Garth stated. "He worked hard, even while the rest of us were goofin' off. I never heard him complain or nothin'. That impressed me."

Joey grinned. "Thanks, Garth. It's easy doin' what you love to do."

"How 'bout you, Ashley?" Ms. Cadena encouraged.

The girl blushed. "I'm kinda embarrassed to say what I'm going to remember most. No one knows about it but me."

"Oh, a mystery!" Ms. Cadena breathed. "Come on, you can tell us."

Ashley glanced over at the couch where Debbie sat snuggled against Wrangler Barry's chest. "It's about them," she said.

Debbie blinked. "Us? Wha'd we do?"

Ashley smiled. "A couple days ago, after everyone had headed for bed, I saw you guys stop at the bottom of the steps."

A smile began to creep across Barry's face. "And?" he prodded.

"And . . . you kissed her. You guys didn't see me, 'cause I was up on the balcony."

Wendy groaned. "That's it? That's your great memory of Shadow Creek Ranch? Man, you should live here. They do it all the time. It's disgusting!"

"No, it's not," Ashley corrected firmly. "I mean, I've seen a lot of kissing. Done some myself." Ms. Cadena cleared her throat. "Well," the girl continued shyly, "maybe I've done a *lot* of it myself, for money usually. But theirs was different. It was gentle and sweet, warm like the embers in a fire." She lowered her eyes. "I'm going to remember it forever."

Debbie reached up and ran her fingers along Barry's cheek. "He's just a gentle and sweet kinda guy," she said affectionately.

"See what I mean?" Wendy moaned.

Luisa giggled. "Well, I didn't see anybody smoochin' from the balcony, but I did do something really incredible. I mean, I fed a mountain lion. That doesn't happen every day unless you work at a zoo. I'm going to think about Monty a lot when I get home, especially . . ." She paused. "Especially when I'm feelin' kinda lonely."

Wendy smiled a warm, encouraging smile. "I'll say 'hello' to him for you every time I go up to his rock formation, OK?"

"OK," Luisa nodded.

Mr. Hanson stretched tired muscles. "I don't know about you guys, but I'm bushed. Y'all wore me out, so I guess I'll head on up to bed. Our guests have an early morning plane to catch, so don't stay up too late. Ms. Cadena will be taking them to the airport in the minivan right after breakfast, so you might want to finish packing before you dive under the covers. G'night everyone. See ya bright and early tomorrow."

"Good night," the young people responded with a wave.

During the next hour conversation around the broad stone hearth began to lag as eyelids grew heavy. One by one, sleepy teenagers stumbled up the steps and dropped into warm, cozy beds while memories, still fresh and alive, replayed in their minds. But soon even they faded as slumber took its toll, replacing memories with dreams.

Wendy lay watching the gray shadows of night creep along her walls. Sleep refused to come, for she knew she'd failed in her plan. Last night she had heard Luisa's moans and cries again, and in just a few moments, midnight would settle over the Station at the chiming of the clock down the hall.

What could she have done differently? What else could she have said to get through to her friend Luisa? She'd carefully guided each conversation around to the subject of fathers and how she loved hers very much. Wasn't that what Dr. Neslund had told her to do? She'd often reminded Luisa of the heaven to come and how she could talk to God and He'd listen to her no matter what she had to say. The same God who was preparing a safe, cheery home for her in a future land of peace, where pain would be long-forgotten.

Now, as midnight approached, she felt discouraged, defeated, and sad.

BONG.

The clock began to chime out the hour.

BONG . . . BONG.

The girl slipped out from under the covers and silently padded to the door.

BONG . . . BONG.

What does it take to tell someone about God, about His love?

BONG . . . BONG.

Is it even possible for a young girl to touch the life of a friend who's hurting?

BONG . . . BONG.

Silently Wendy crept down the long hallway, a great sorrow making her footsteps heavy.

BONG . . . BONG . . . BONG.

The clock fell silent. Wendy listened. Sure enough, the unmistakable sounds of someone moaning rose behind the closed door leading into Luisa's room. The girl slid down until she was sitting on the cold, wooden floor, her head resting against the jam. What more could she have done?

Then Wendy looked up sharply as she recognized one of the words drifting in the still night air. Pressing her ear firmly against the door she waited, listening.

". . . and I'm scared, God. I'm scared," the unseen speaker was saying. "Can You help me?"

Wendy's eyes opened wide as her breath caught in her throat.

"I want to live in heaven where there's no more pain. Could You build me a house next to Wendy? She's a real friend and cares about me. I know she does because she took me to see Monty. She understands what's in my heart, and listens when I talk—really listens. Please, may I live next to her in heaven?"

Still sitting outside the door, Wendy pressed her hands against her face as sudden tears spilled down her cheeks.

"And God," she heard the girl moan, "help my mom. Help her to be kinder to me and not . . . and not hurt me so much. I'm going to tell Captain Grant everything, so if You can kinda show him what to do for me and my family, I'd appreciate it.

"That's all I have to say. I hope I did it right. Amen."

Out in the hallway Wendy remained motionless, face buried in her hands. In the stillness of the midnight hour, as the other occupants of Shadow Creek Ranch slept the deep sleep of peace, she whispered a private response to the girl's prayer. Then, in a voice only God could hear, she said, "Amen."

❄ ❄ ❄

Joey fidgeted in his desk chair. The Station was strangely quiet as he turned the object over and over in his hands. The guests had gone amid smiles, handshakes, and hugs right after breakfast, leaving him with the sad, lonely feeling that occurs whenever friends depart.

Now the bright afternoon sun shone through his

downstairs window striking the strange gift with a brilliant beam as if highlighting the problem.

"I know, I know," he mumbled to himself. "She's on her way, and I still haven't the faintest idea what this gizmo is for."

He heard footsteps in the hallway. "Joey?" a young girl called. "Are you in your room?"

"Yeah, Sam," he responded.

The footsteps grew nearer.

"What's it for? *What's it for?*" the boy gasped, looking wildly around the room as if expecting the answer to pop out of nowhere.

He could hear Samantha's booted feet clunking past the dining room. "Hope it's the right color for your *new* pencils," he heard her say in his mind.

Pencils? *New* pencils? Joey's hands shook. The holes. The holes are for pencils! He grabbed a handful of them and jammed them into the openings drilled in not-so-neat rows along the top of the object.

"And where should pencils be kept?" he whispered hoarsely. "On the desk!" He slammed the wooden object down on top of a pile of papers resting at one corner of his writing table just as Samantha burst into the room. She smiled over at her adopted brother. "What did you want to see me about?" she asked cheerily.

Joey cleared his throat. "Ah . . . I just wanted to thank you for this." He pointed at his gift. "It's the best . . . ah . . . pencil holder/paper weight I've ever received, and I mean that."

Samantha nodded. "You're welcome." Then she looked at his head. "Why are you wearing your hat inside your bedroom. Isn't your head hot?"

"Kinda."

"So, hang it on the hook."

"The hook?"

The little girl giggled. "You're trickin' me again, aren't you, Joey?" She paused at the door. "Well?"

Joey slowly reached up and removed his broad-rimmed, leather riding hat. "Sure," he said. "I'll just put it on . . . on . . ."

Suddenly the answer sparked in his brain like a lightbulb flickering to life. "On the hook," he said, reaching over and placing his hat on the long nail jutting out from the side of his desk, the nail Samantha had firmly hammered into her gift. Joey smiled in victory. "This is the best pencil holder/paper weight/hat rack I've ever seen. Thanks, Sam."

The little girl beamed. "Hey, Joey, you're pretty smart. Wendy couldn't figure out how to use hers. Had to show her and everything. See ya."

The boy's mouth dropped open as he fell back against his chair. Wendy hadn't known either? But she . . . she . . .

"WEN—DY!"

The call echoed about the Station like the cry of some wild animal on the hunt. But the object of Joey's determined summons wasn't around to

157

hear it. She was sitting alone, staring down at Shadow Creek Ranch from her distant perch on the overlook.

The cold wind shook the dead leaves, rattling the forest behind her like a medicine man's charm. Chin in hands, she studied the valley in silence. She didn't even hear her father approaching from behind until he spoke.

"I thought I'd find you up here," he called to her, maneuvering around the rocks forming the lip of the overlook. "Aren't you cold?"

"When did she leave?" the girl asked without turning around.

"Your mother left just after lunch. Grandpa drove her to the airport."

Wendy glanced up at her dad as he settled himself beside her. "She didn't even say good-bye."

Mr. Hanson nodded. "I know. She said she didn't want to make a scene. Insisted she'd start crying and stuff and would embarrass everyone, so she just left quietly, the same way she came."

Wendy felt her father's arm wrap around her narrow shoulders. "Are you OK, sweetheart?"

The girl suppressed a quiet sob. "Will she come back?"

Mr. Hanson rested his chin on the girl's head. "She said she might. Maybe in a year or so. Maybe longer."

"Dad?"

"Yes."

"Why are some people so . . . so restless?"

The man gazed down at Shadow Creek Ranch, his heart breaking for the little girl in his arms. "They just are," he said softly, trying to control his own emotions. "Some people don't know how to be still and live life the way it is. They always want things to be different, to be more like their dreams. Reality kinda throws 'em, I guess."

He heard Wendy sigh. "I'm not going to be like that," the girl stated, her voice shaking. "I'm going to love someone no matter what happens, even if things aren't exactly like I want them to be. Isn't that the way to do it?"

Mr. Hanson fought back tears. "Yes, sweetheart. That's the way it should be. That's the way God loves us."

The two sat watching the winds send swirls of snow across the pastures and meadows below.

"By the way," he said, brightening, "I've got a date tonight."

"You do?"

"Yup. I'm taking Ruth to a fancy restaurant in Bozeman and then we're going to go to the university for a concert. Gonna wear a suit and everything! Wanna come?"

Wendy looked up at her dad. "You and Ms. Cadena aren't going to get all mushy like Debbie and Barry, are you?"

"Maybe."

The girl shook her head and let out a frustrated sigh. "What's this world coming to?" she asked. "Can't go 10 feet without bumpin' into somebody lovin' someone. How embarrassing!"

Mr. Hanson grabbed his daughter and lifted her up, pulling her away from the overlook. "It's a conspiracy against all the Wendys in the world," he growled, carrying her giggling, squirming form toward the forest path. "We just want to make your lives miserable."

The girl squealed and laughed, fighting off the man's hugs. "And you'll probably be wearing tons of that silly perfume," she said.

"Aftershave. Men wear aftershave. Women wear perfume."

Breaking free, Wendy ran ahead of her father, and the two of them vanished into the forest. From the shadows came, "Well, I don't want to smell like a flower or a tree. I'm happy to stink like Early."

The man laughed. "How romantic."

Soon the only sound heard at the overlook was the blowing wind. High above, farther than the laughter of Shadow Creek Ranch could reach, an airliner sailed through the blue afternoon sky.

One passenger, a woman with soft blond hair, sat with face pressed against the window, gazing down at the white folds of land passing slowly far below. Her lips moved, forming her farewell to the girl she knew lived among the mountains. In words torn from her heart, she whispered, "Goodbye, Wendy."